A Favorable Match

Butterton
Brides
Book 2

Ann Elizabeth Fryer

For my Regency-loving friend, Kelly Hall,
who long ago understood and shared my passion for all things
Jane.

CHAPTER ONE

London, England

January, 1810

How strange to think that I, Lady Emma Bartlett, have never enjoyed a London Season. Ever. I had greatly desired a Season of my very own when I was much younger—so eager to burst from this cocoon, try my wings, and alight softly but stunningly upon the many fancy balls and soirees available to one such as I. But Season after Season passed, without Grandfather allowing me to debut or even be merely presented at court. Never mind that I've lived in the thick of such doings my entire life.

Already aged twenty and one, I would feel a spinster among the newly blossomed sixteen-year-olds, whose fresher complexions and eager guardians would far outshine my own entourage.

Grandfather and my twin great uncles had been my sole parentage for most of my life, indeed, they have been my dearest protectors—as a high iron fence around me, armed with spears to threaten – and maim – any gentleman who might attempt to scale it.

As the years slowly passed, I had quite given up on having a Season or any sort of pleasant pursuit outside of these walls, grand though they are. I would be a companion to my grandfather and great uncles. Pour tea for them. And maybe, if Grandfather was in a good mood, he would lower the weapons to receive the rare visitor. That Grandfather himself had the gall to bring up my lack of Seasons and my failure to meet a suitable mate, yet again, irritated.

"A Season." Grandfather spat. "I'll not be caught dead playing "dear Mama" to our *dear* Emma." He sent a smile in my direction. "Like a biddy-hen showing off her chick? I think not." He took a bite of toast and chewed heartily while speaking. "She is too priceless for such treatment."

I tapped my spoon atop my poached egg. The shell cracked. Grandfather's good intentions shattered with little effort. Too times many to count.

Uncle Richard chimed in. "No, indeed. A duke is certainly not a "mama-hen"." A giggle raced up his throat, his mutton chop beard quivering as he munched bacon.

"Quite so, quite so." Uncle Gerald tented his fingers and peered over his glasses. "But one might hire a lady to do the job. Mrs. Norris, perhaps. It has been done before, you know."

Such an early hour to be discussing my courtship and ultimate matrimony. As per usual, the talk would go nowhere, and neither would I.

"Emma is not a job, Gerald." Grandfather brushed buttery toast crumbs from his dressing gown, making another mess for someone else. "Ridiculous. I would trust no one to satisfactorily accomplish such a venture, Mrs. Norris, notwithstanding. She hasn't the energy for it." He pointed his butter knife like the finger of caution. "They'll be after our money, brothers. And we mustn't let them anywhere near it. Our Emma will inherit a great fortune someday. In the interim, we must take precipitous care as to the intentions of her suitors."

Uncle Richard stabbed the air with his fork. "I'll pierce the scoundrel."

As though the family silver alone might protect my heart.

"Cloudy day today." Uncle Gerald reached for the newspaper, but Grandfather snatched it first.

"Mmm."

The conversation went in another direction with nary a blink between subjects. The silverware returned to regular usage, and I returned to my egg.

Grandfather opened the front page. "Oh my." He looked up from the words. "Listen here, brothers. It says that Banbury—is dead."

Uncle Gerald laid down his napkin, mouth open. "The old rapscallion."

Uncle Richard echoed Gerald, "The scallion."

Uncle Gerald rolled his eyes. "He isn't an onion."

Richard smirked. "Wasn't, dear brother. Wasn't."

Grandfather pointed to the print. "Before anyone could see justice served, too. My, my, my."

The room grew silent, and what little light there was peeking through the east-facing windows of the breakfast room grew dimmer. Thick clouds gathered and the candles in the middle of the small, round table glowed all the brighter.

Grandfather spoke in the sudden, eerie stillness. "You recall he tried to kill me when we were but lads." He was very matter-of-fact.

Kill him? My uncles nodded in unison.

"Grandfather?" Nearly *murdered*? "What's this? Surely not." Egg yolk slipped from my spoon and into a gooey puddle on my napkin. *Lovely.*

He took a deep breath and shook his still handsome, silvered head. "Had I not survived, you would not exist. 'Tis a sorry tale, but I will tell it."

Uncle Richard raised a brow. "The short version, mind you. Given the present company."

Meaning myself, of course. Was the story too sordid for my feminine ears?

"Ah. Right you are." Grandfather took another sip of tea and began. "Your—my—" He hesitated. "It's no use. I can't tell it properly."

Uncle Gerald laid his hands flat on the table. "I will give it a try."

"Thank you, brother."

His lips turned down as if tasting the truth and finding it unpleasant. "You see, Banbury and your dearly departed grandmother—I um, that is to say..."

I had never met my grandmother, and here, at last, there was a hint of intrigue.

Uncle Gerald continued. "He pursued her, and she rejected him. There."

Grandfather picked the story back up again. "She was already engaged to marry me, you understand. And I couldn't swim." Again, a fact stated.

"You couldn't swim?" Surely, he had a further point to make.

"To my shame."

I failed to see what that had to do with anything. Grandfather had aged considerably in the last few years. Sometimes, I worried about his wandering mind...

"I'm making a muck of the thing. See here, Emma," Grandfather swept his hand across the table, knocking over the salt cellar. "Banbury pushed me into the Thames, laughing as he did so." He leaned forward. "Never a more evil man."

"The rapscallion," Uncle Gerald repeated.

Grandfather picked up the salt cellar and set it aright, but held onto the tiny silver spoon. "Chinworth rescued me. Remember that? Good ole Chinworth..." His voice faded and his attention caught on a remembrance of something the rest of us couldn't see. Grandfather stood. "Chinworth may well be the answer to our predicament." He smiled and rested his eyes on me. "Poor thing. Don't know why I didn't think of it before."

Uncle Gerald and Richard's eyes brightened as they spoke in unison. "Excellent idea!"

"What?" I was at a complete loss. What predicament did he speak about? Is that how they saw me? As purely problematic?

The quiet three gazed at me with tender expressions. As though they'd become increasingly sentimental as my birthday came 'round each year. What did I have to do with Grandfather's dunk in the Thames? Was *I* the predicament? How so?

The air in the room filled with expectation and dread. When they walked out together, I felt as though I heard the death knell. But for what, I didn't know. Why had they acted so strangely? What in the heavens did he refer to?

For a month, I wouldn't discover the reason. January slipped into February and the name of Chinworth died on their lips. I went on as before, despite the strange glances they'd shared. Obviously, a secret whispered betwixt them, one not meant for my ears.

So, I tried to ignore the change in their behavior towards me. I stitched two new cushions, poured lots of tea at tea time, read books about people who did things and went places...until one afternoon, I'd had enough of the stifling indoor air.

I threw my stitchery and books aside and took a walk to church. The weather had been too cold recently, and I hadn't been outside for days. Fresh air was often a cure for boredom. At least that was my hope.

I couldn't go far, but Grandfather wouldn't object to me paying respects at my parents' grave. I tried to avoid whispers among those whom I passed along the way. *Lady Emma, the prisoner. Lady Emma, her fortune. Lady Emma, not out...* Wide bonnets could not buffer busy tongues. I recognized many faces but knew none of them.

My maid and footman closed in on each side of me as if to stifle the gossip. Was I a prisoner? The Ton simply didn't understand. I wasn't on the marriage market because Grandfather was loathe to share his fortune with any man who might sully the Bartlett name by losing at the tables. A winner, of course, he mightn't mind. Bet if I'd been a grandson, they wouldn't be so careful about attachments.

Besides, my grandfather didn't like to part with money—not even a half pence. But surely not all gentlemen gambled? Surely there was a man in existence that could love me with or without the fortune. Was that so unthinkable?

In truth, my personal prison was my inheritance. A terrible thought forced its way to the surface as the graveyard came into view. Grandfather must die before I truly inherited. Sad truth.

I blinked once, then twice. Even if I had a fortune under my control, would I be free? Would I give myself a Season among the ton? Would I allow suitor after suitor through the doors of Chatswick House? Dress in glamorous ballgowns and dance the night away on the arms of assorted handsome men? I laughed audibly and clapped a hand over my mouth. Grandfather would rise from the grave to stop such silliness before I made a complete fool of myself. Or lost every coin. I was sure of it.

Tessa looked at me sideways while the footman raised a brow. "Did someone tell a joke? I missed it."

"I was thinking how ridiculous it would be to give myself a Season in Town."

Tessa chided. "Losh, but he keeps you under lock and key, doesn't he?"

The footman opened the front gate. "For good reason, Miss." He stopped me with a hand to my arm, his kindly blue eyes full of sympathy. "The staff feels for you, me and my Mrs. especially.

A young bright one such as yourself shouldn't be trapped with three dusty old codgers who'd rather stay home with their pipes and newspapers."

Tessa grew solemn. "I pray for you night and day, Lady Emma."

While appreciative, I didn't know what to say. The staff had never dared be so forward before. A surprising warmth filled my heart. As if the shackles of rank that separated us fell away. "Thank you—both of you."

I made my way into the cemetery, down a pebbled path that veered to the right, near a single yew tree, an evergreen symbol of life and hope. A striking contrast to the winter-barren trees that slept before waking again to offer the mourner shade from the hot sun.

One shared stone stood in place. The granite memorial rose tall, topped with an ornate marble bowl of fruit. I touched the cold apples and grapes. Traced the vines whose tendrils led down to their chiseled names. They'd died in an accident when I was an infant. Such a devastating loss. Nineteen years without them, my memories empty except for a mere scrap. I remember being warm and held, and then, a great emptiness. Unending. How I grieved that emptiness.

I knelt to brush away debris from the previous night's storm before offering my hothouse flowers. I faltered. There, on the gravestone, were two coins. Strange. Each perfectly centered beneath their names.

Someone had been here recently.

Who? And why? Grandfather and my uncles never ventured here. Only I remained to pause and care.

I looked about. The footman waved from his place by the gate. Tessa paid her respects to another set of graves. I glanced back at the coins. I supposed I should leave them and let the caretaker do what he would with the offering. I added my bouquet. Though I couldn't remember my parents, I never wanted to forget that I'd once belonged to them. That they loved me.

A movement shifted on the other side of the yew. A black coat, top hat. A young man stood nearby, at another grave. I caught a flick of his eyes. Had he been watching me? I felt instantly uncomfortable. How had I not noticed? He bowed to me, then left.

My footman was quickly at my elbow, staring after the man. "Must've been in the church. He didn't bother you, did he, Miss?"

"Of course not."

I wouldn't have thought about it again had we not passed the same gentleman on the way home. He tipped his hat to me. A friendly gesture but too familiar, too audacious of him! I turned against the heat that rose unbidden to my cheeks.

Only his expression did not appear as if he were trying to catch my eye—as some men had tried before. Instead, he seemed concerned. The wrinkle between his brows squeezed together, his lips pressed with purpose. *He has mistaken me for someone else. Yes, that must be it.* Likely, I'd never see him again.

When we returned to Chatswick, I lay aside my cloak and bonnet and made my way to the library where, it seemed, I must live vicariously through the adventures of others, find escape between the pages of my many novels.

Tessa handed me a message. I scanned the words. Mrs. Norris had canceled supper and cards tonight—the kind, and rather aged aristocratic woman and her daughters were the only approved friendships I had outside of home. Grandfather was strict about my connections. They had come down with sore throats and lay abed sipping honey tea. Poor things. I could rest assured that I would be reinvited the week after next. I snatched my shawl from the chair and flung it about my shoulders.

Hannah and Isabel, the Miss Norris's, were spinsters, well over one hundred twenty years between them. It was said that Hannah's intended had sadly died in the American colonies many years ago. The tragedy had bound the sisters together, and together they stayed. "Tis safe to remain in one's own home and not go traipsing about," the widow once said. Indeed. Mrs. Norris and Grandfather were of one mind. Isabel was one of God's children as well, and an expert at cards. Amazingly, she always won. Always.

Just as well. I sat in the chair and opened my current journey. Closed it again. No. A novel wasn't enough. The pain of my solitude pressed on me as never before. The footman's kind concern about my life unsteadied me.

I loved this home, but oh, how I wanted to leap beyond its doors and see the world. How dare I entertain such thoughts? No sooner had the rogue desire formed within my mind than I was summoned to Grandfather's study. Uncle Gerald dabbed his eyes with a handkerchief, Uncle Richard tried his best to retain composure.

"Whatever is the matter?" I turned to Grandfather who had the widest smile I'd ever seen upon his face. In his hand, a letter.

"I knew Chinworth would come through!"

Chinworth—the man who had fished Grandfather from the Thames and ensured my existence. Was the mystery finally to be revealed?

"You are to be congratulated, my dear, for you shall travel and spend the spring and summer at his estate." He wrapped an arm around my shoulder. "I trust no one more than Chinworth! Good ole fellow!"

I wasn't sure I heard him correctly. "I don't understand." I was leaving Chatswick? And London? To do what?

My uncles laughed in unison.

"Chinworth has three sons, and you shall have the pick of them! They all remain as yet unmarried." His ridiculous grin widened as though it were Christmas and he'd given me the moon. My stomach squeezed.

Uncle Richard pulled a chair for me to sit—how weak my knees had grown!

"Surely you do not mean for me to marry one of them?" Mortification barely began to describe my emotions.

Grandfather set the letter down and his smile faltered. "Indeed, I do."

"But we don't know them, I—"

"My dear," he took my hand, "Any offspring Chinworth has produced will most certainly be of the highest quality—of this you must not doubt."

Uncle Gerald wagged three fingers in the air. "We had to provide you with quality options, my dear."

What a plan! A woman did not simply pick a husband. Not in this way. How uncouth. "I would rather hope a man would choose me instead..." I was completely taken off my guard. Befuddled.

The three old gentlemen surrounded me, pride showing in their lined faces. "Who could refuse such beauty and intellect?" Grandfather grinned.

Who, indeed?

At present, my fortune trapped me. Would these bonds ever set me free?

CHAPTER TWO

Another month went by before I again saw the stranger in the graveyard. He bent his head in acknowledgment but did not approach. I felt his eyes alight upon me. Gentlemen had stared so before, but I'd learned to ignore their glances. I tamped down my own curiosity with an iron resolve. The footman, thankfully, was never far away. I felt safe.

I shifted behind the yew tree but he moved to another headstone and I was once more in his full view. The man caught my stare as his hand rose—he glanced at the footman and back to me. I quickly looked away. Did he desire to speak? He would have to go through proper channels. Like all the others. Little did he know that the way would be barred, as it was with every other gentleman. I walked home with a sliver of unease. Never had anyone been so curious about me.

My impending travel to Butterton to meet the Chinworth trio became a daily chore and most assuredly, a frightening prospect. But I have to admit I was curious about those young men. And also anxious. Though I'd had a good governess stuff me full of the social graces, I'd never had enough practice at the actual task. No real experience.

Mrs. Grayson, having fulfilled her duties toward me, was recommended to another family of five daughters that lived far from London. I missed her terribly. She'd been gone for two long years. A void the Norris's couldn't fill.

I stood on a low stool as the seamstress put the final hem in my latest gown.

"And that does it my lady. If I may say so, this green brings out your eyes."

"I thank you."

She helped me down and turned me in front of the mirror. Never did I own anything so fashionable. "It's a work of art, Mrs. Hampton." But would the Chinworth brothers like it?

Tessa came behind me and agreed. "Finest dress I ever laid eyes on. Truly, it is!" She plucked a stray thread from my shoulder. "Your grandfather asks you to attend him in the drawing room."

I made my way down the steps and through the corridor. Why the drawing room? He usually spent his days in either the breakfast parlor or study. I slipped into the gracious room filled with my grandmother's things. Faded yellow silk-covered walls, statues of dogs flanked the cold fireplace, and a rather garish red velvet covered the furniture made to accommodate much wider dresses than the current fashion.

"Chinworth sends another letter, my dear." Grandfather took my hand to view me better and smiled with approval. "'Tis a good thing your wardrobe is ready. Yes, indeed, for he writes begging me to hasten your arrival."

"Does he?" Nerves built. My desire to see the world collided with his plan for me to choose a husband. The trip would be a diversion, yes, but I couldn't fathom this working in my favor. Or that of the gentlemen in question either. The possibilities unnerved me. Not that I had another way to see the world...without Grandfather's provision.

If only I had the chance to be around a few civil men on a trial outing. Grow accustomed to groups of people, parties. And, of course, dances. *Dances.* I cringed. I should be happier about the prospect. Instead, my inadequacies berated me. I daresay I wouldn't remember the steps that Mrs. Grayson tried to teach me. I knew what would happen. I'd stomp on toes and humiliate myself—

Grandfather's voice cut into my vain panic. "Indeed. Even now, Chinworth is anxious to meet you. I cannot blame him."

I was to depart the first of April. Another full month to get used to the idea. To practice moving across the dance floor. "How much sooner does he expect me?"

"He is such a gracious host, my love, that he awaits you even now." He raised an eyebrow. "With open arms."

"Now?" Impossible. "I'm afraid I must decline to better prepare..." Grandfather must understand. Had to. I wasn't ready.

"Nonsense, your gowns are ready, are they not? What more do you need?" He smiled. "You've no reason to delay." He patted my hand and bent low. "It is alright, dear Emma. This is a big step. It is natural to be nervous."

"Gowns aren't my objection—I—"

A startling shadow moved in the doorway, then entered the room. The man from the graveyard. I swallowed at his unexpected presence. Bereft of the long, dark coat, here stood before me a gentleman of sorts. His frame, though not towering, appeared strong, his brown eyes snapped a perusal of me. I stepped back as though he were an intruder.

Grandfather turned to greet him. "Yes, do come in, Mr. Carter. Be introduced to my granddaughter."

I managed to curtsy while he bowed. "Mr. Carter. A pleasure to make your acquaintance." He showed no sign of our brief encounters. Dare I mention them?

"Mr. Carter is Chinworth's nephew." Grandfather's smile widened. "He's been commissioned to escort us to Mayfield Manor. Such kindness, I daresay. Such kindness."

Nephew? How strange. "Indeed. How thoughtful." I didn't know what else to say.

"An honor to meet you, Miss Bartlett, and my pleasure to serve you." He bowed again. His trim, sandy-brown hair swept to the side, and somewhat sharp, thin features combined into a handsome visage—excepting the jagged scar at his ear. I wondered how he'd acquired it.

Where were my manners? "Please be seated." I motioned towards the chairs and lowered to the settee.

Grandfather pulled the bell.

Oh no. I'd forgotten to ring for tea, but I would not forget to pour.

"Dear me," Grandfather stood again and patted his jacket as though feeling for a cigar. "I must retrieve your uncles."

He left the room and propriety behind. I'd never been alone with any gentlemen except my family members. Not once. How could he put me in such a tenuous position? It simply wasn't done. I fished for something to say. Anything. Perhaps propriety demanded that I leave the room also. I rose, but he reached out for me. I shifted farther into my chair, allowing my back to lean in ever so slightly.

He spoke, his voice low. "How fortuitous that we are alone."

Gone was his polished manner. So, he *had* wanted to talk to me that day. Yet I shrunk from his words. "Is it? How so?"

He scooted to the edge of his chair and tented his hands. "Miss Bartlett, I must insist upon discretion. What I have to say isn't pleasant." His voice lowered.

Perhaps I would discover why he was following me at the graveyard.

He continued. "Uncle will be furious with me, but, Miss Bartlett, I must beg you to reconsider your visit."

"Reconsider my visit? I don't understand."

"Don't go to Mayfield. I beg your trust." He stared at me with bold, brown eyes. "It's for your own good."

Mr. Carter rose to his feet and so did I. Heat flushed through my body, head to toe. Trust a man I didn't know? I was no fool. What manner of request was this?

He pressed his lips together and took in a deep breath. "My warning is kindly meant. I care for my uncle, but I can't see someone like you—"

He was cut off. Grandfather returned with Uncle Gerald and Richard. What had he been about to say? *Someone like me...?* Me, the heiress? Me, the strange girl raised by three old gentlemen? I could feel the ruby in my cheeks.

Laughter and smiles filled the room as introductions were made and the trio reminisced about school days with Chinworth—and Mr. Carter's own father.

Neither of us shared the memories and so could only sip our tea, pretending to be interested in the many disjointed stories. Some quite strange. All the while, Mr. Carter's warning prodded within the occasional glances he sent my way, as though he tried to whisper within my mind. I couldn't help being curious about his concerns.

His manners at the graveyard at once confused and enlightened me. He'd wanted to tell me then. Of course. But why not come forward? Why wait until now? A chill slipped up my spine. How had he known I'd be there in the first place? My visits weren't regular or planned.

If he had such objections concerning my visit to Mayfield Manor, shouldn't he discuss such worries with Grandfather? Why the hesitation? If something was amiss, the old gentleman should be told directly. Perhaps Mr. Carter would wait until he had a private audience.

Dutifully, I refilled tea cups and handed around the plate of cake.

Grandfather clapped his hands together. "You'll stay here, of course. Emma and I shall be ready in no less than two days. Two days! Think of it, Richard and Gerald. Haven't left this house since...well...at any rate, I feel a youthfulness about my bones. A spring in my step. Anything could happen!"

Anything could happen indeed.

Mr. Carter stood. "You are too kind. I thank you."

I was so very confused.

Uncle Gerald drained his cup and plied him. "And what of your father? Wyndhouse still standing?"

Mr. Carter's lips quirked. "Father travels to Scotland to help a friend with his estate and Wyndhouse stands yet. For how long, I cannot predict." A quiet laugh followed his words.

I surmised his estate to be a near ruin. Something in his voice...

Grandfather clattered teacup to saucer. "Chinworth will see you well-set, I shouldn't wonder."

Mr. Carter didn't reply. Nor did he try to dissuade Grandfather from delivering me to Mayfield Manor. *Someone like me*, he'd said. Perhaps I didn't fit the expectation of not being out in society. How unkind to comment upon my lack of polish.

I didn't know what else to make of it. I took my leave and found Tessa already organizing my trunks.

I was a mix of warring emotions. As a prisoner about to escape, I knew that I mustn't remain here, or I would burst. The practical side knew that if I went, I'd never be the same. I would be leaving home for the first time in my life. Regardless of what happened, I would finally be learning about the ways of the world. Books, however diverting, could never replace real experience. I hoped fervently that this was true.

Perhaps this Mr. Carter had his own agenda with Chinworth and thought my presence would get in the way. His strange behavior at the graveyard, and our conversation begged solid answers. At least Grandfather would travel with me. I took great solace in that. If anything was truly amiss, we would return to Chatswick. But after such a tour, would we ever go on as before?

I placed a hand across my eyes as a headache surged. My stomach squeezed. The strain of the sudden changes stirred my nerves. I rubbed my head.

"Are you unwell, my lady?" Tessa pressed a wet handkerchief to my temples.

"Do you still pray for me, Tessa?" I looked her in the eyes.

"Aye, that I do."

"Please continue."

"Of course, of course. Why don't you lie down until supper," She guided me to the bed, "and I'll sit beside you and pray while you rest."

I'd learned to petition the Lord from my governess. Memorized prayers. I'd read prayers in novels—prayed by heroes and heroines in dire need. As I lay across my comfortable bed, my strain and anxiety seemed ludicrous compared to what others had endured. Yet I couldn't help feeling that if someone wasn't praying for me, these foreign, troubled emotions would worsen. My panic would grow—and I would truly never leave and see anything of the world...*Hear Tessa's prayer, God. I know not what to pray...*

Dinner was a better affair than I expected. Grandfather's jolly mood put me at ease, and my uncles joined in laughter, sometimes giving me an impression of the boys they'd once been. Mr. Carter himself was all politeness, seemingly taking on an aura of peace. Maybe even surrender. Perhaps he'd given up on dissuading me from my journey. As though I had a choice either way.

I ate my meal, my earlier headache all but gone.

Grandfather plied Mr. Carter. "How are you employed by our friend Chinworth, lad?"

"I'm his general assistant. His estate is large—there is much opportunity to learn, as I plan to return to Wyndhouse and make the land profitable."

"Well done, then."

"Thank you. I will also see to Matthew Dawe's training. He is Banbury's heir."

"Heir?" Uncle Gerald sputtered, looking intently at the others. Uncle Richard dropped his knife to the floor.

Grandfather's brows rose. "He had no children, no relatives to inherit..."

"He did, after all." Mr. Carter nodded.

"Rapscallion like his father, I shouldn't wonder." Uncle Richard's lips grew tight. "Dawes, did you say? Not of Dawes Shipping, I do hope. Nasty business, that."

"It is Banbury's grandson who survives—"

Grandfather coughed behind his napkin. "A grandson, is it? I daresay his father was born on the wrong side of the blanket."

Mr. Carter's jaw grew tight. "Having been introduced to the lad, I can assure you that we have great hopes for him."

"We?" Grandfather's silver brows rose.

"Lord Sherborne and I."

"Lord Sherborne—the gentleman who saw to Banbury's downfall, eh? Good man."

"The same."

Uncle Richard popped a bit of beef into his mouth, chewing and talking simultaneously. "And what sea did he fish the lad from?"

Mr. Carter scooted his peas away from the roasted carrots on his plate. As though dividing one thought from another. The boy from the terrible man? "The Cornish Sea, if you must know. Banbury nearly killed him. We are thankful that the young gentleman lives."

Grandfather sat in quiet thought for a moment, neither eating nor drinking. "I didn't take you for a tutor—not one of your station."

"A tutor? No indeed. I shall teach him to fight and shoot. Necessary lessons should he ever be accosted again."

Banbury had nearly killed Grandfather too. I wondered at this man of wealth and rank who would stoop to wound his own flesh and blood. Such evil was impossible to fathom.

"Adept with the sword and pistol, are you?" Grandfather smiled again, glancing my way. "We shall be well protected on our journey, Emma."

Unpleasant conversation behind us, the gentlemen returned to their beefsteaks in hungry silence, not noticing Mr. Carter's gaze upon me. He studied me for more than a moment. Wondering how to be rid of us, I shouldn't wonder.

What a difference one conversation can make.

CHAPTER THREE

I burned the midnight oil sorting through things to pack. Books I could not do without, which gloves to keep and which to donate to charity. Tessa had gone to bed hours ago and I found that I was too energetic, too anxious to sleep. Footsteps padded past my bedroom door. Who did they belong to?

For the first time for as long as I can recall, I'd locked it after Tessa retired for the evening. I didn't trust the stranger and thought I might sleep better knowing his entry was barred. His advice and gazes had set me on edge. My heart pounded and I swallowed. The handle to the door did not move as I expected. Instead, a quiet shuffling sounded. A message thrust through the gap. From Mr. Carter? Had to be.

I stood still, hardly able to breathe, unable to move until his footsteps faded down the hall. Snatching the missive from the ground, I unfolded the words. Never had I received a message, and never in such a secretive manner.

Miss Bartlett,

Please forgive me. We couldn't have the quiet conversation I had hoped for. I do not desire to go against my uncle or your grandfather—truly—I cannot. As I'm unable to stop you from attending Mayfield for the summer. Perhaps I can persuade you to stay at Chatswick of your own volition? My reasons are genuine, though I am loathe to pen them on this paper. I dare think the actual situation would surprise you. I would speak to you in private—please meet me at the graveyard at 10 am on the morrow? I will be waiting to explain.

Respectfully,

Joseph Carter

Undeniably. We must have words, this Joseph Carter and I. Earlier, he spoke of some unpleasantness. Now he speaks of loathing. If he would but relay the situation, clearly and distinctly, I could indeed make a proper determination. As it was, he'd told me nothing. His words were a cryptic warning, and the more I thought about it, it was outright odd that he would choose to meet at the graveyard. Why there of all places? Possibly he too had loved ones buried in the sacred place? Perhaps I should simply ask him, but that would be impertinent.

I decided I should hear what he had to say. Meet him. The questions he posed begged an answer.

I tossed the note into the fire as a cry echoed down the hall. A voice shouted, several footsteps pounded—what was happening? I threw on my robe and joined them—at Grandfather's door.

He writhed in pain on the floor as his manservant and a footman knelt by his side. "Fire, oh the fire. It hurts me so."

"Grandfather?" Panic swelled.

His pale face stretched with pain. "I suffer, Emma, oh I suffer!" His nightcap hung askew over one ear as he arched his back in a cry.

His manservant motioned for me to leave. "It's his gout, my lady."

I hadn't realized the malady had progressed—he used to call it a "mere trifling" pain. This obviously was far more.

"I'll be sending for the doctor." They carefully lifted him back upon his bed. "There's nothing you can do, we will take good care of him."

Mr. Carter stood in the dark hallway, jacketless and hair mussed. "Is he alright?"

I looked back at Grandfather, whose form agonized in the shadows. He seemed so much older. I closed the door behind me and tightened my robe, uncertain. I didn't want to leave his side.

The manservant hurried past. Mr. Carter awaited my response.

What could I say? "I pray he will be well by morning."

Mr. Carter bowed. "Yes, I pray so. Goodnight, Miss Bartlett."

It was not to be.

I woke to the news that his pain was so crippling that he would not be journeying to Mayfield. I would be going alone, with Tessa as my companion. And Mr. Carter, of course, whom I hadn't seen the entire morning.

Grandfather patted my hand. "There, there. You're a grown woman, and I have no doubt of Chinworth's character. You will do us proud, I know." He tried to smile but faltered. "Your carriage leaves very early in the morning. Use this day wisely, my dear."

He'd been so looking forward to the trip. I knew it must rankle him to bow out. "I cannot possibly think of going without you. We will wait out your illness and go together." I had to insist. It was the right thing to do, plus I sought anything to delay my arrival.

He shook his head, the tassel on his nightcap swinging. "I would have left you there after a week, regardless."

I did not want to be abandoned. "But Grandfather. I was rather depending on you to at least look over the gentlemen you desire me to choose from. Can they be as good as you suppose?" His thoughts mattered to me.

His hand gripped mine all the tighter. "The Chinworth family never raised a fool. Impossible."

"Can we not delay our trip until you are well?" I had to try. "Please let me help care for you."

"And keep Chinworth waiting? I think not. Would be rude, after our many years of friendship." He swallowed and gasped at the pain. "My tonic, dear."

I handed him a small glass jar from the side table, of an apothecary I'd not heard of. He snatched it eagerly and downed half of its contents. This liquid he didn't seem to much mind.

He smacked his lip and his eyes fluttered. "I am especially grateful he's sent Mr. Carter to us. He will keep you and Tessa safe. I know he will. Good lad, Carter...he'll keep you..." His voice trailed off, his eyes blinked. "I'm tired, Emma."

His eyes closed and the remaining liquid in the tipped jar dribbled onto his blanket. The tonic's power subdued him quickly, took it from his slack hands.

I drew his blanket around his shoulders, adjusted his cap to cover his ears, and took the aging hand in my own. This man meant the world to me. He'd spoiled me as a child. Gave me everything. Dolls, dresses, tea sets, as many books as I desired. I only had to name an object and he'd have it delivered without discussion.

My governess had much to undo when she came to teach me. Thanks to Grandfather. She helped show me that what became important was no longer an item, but a person. People. Of whom I'd little contact with excepting my family.

Things would always be easy to give. But not this. Not friendships, alliances, a spouse—an entirely different exchange that money couldn't buy. Grandfather couldn't barter with emotions. With my uncles only was he entirely faithful.

Belongings and things were predictable and solid. People were volatile and set him on edge. Especially when someone disagreed. I couldn't help but wonder if we were poor, would we have more friends? And if Chinworth was such a good friend, then why had I never met him? Most titled gentlemen made trips to London a few times each year. A meeting wouldn't have been impossible.

Because of this, I questioned why Grandfather was so anxious to see me wed and settled after locking me away from society for what essentially was my whole life. I thought back to the day when it all began. An opened newspaper, and a memory of a rescue...

Grandfather's hand twitched as the small clock on the mantelpiece chimed. Was nearly ten o'clock. I must walk to the kirk with haste. But whatever would I discover?

The Ton must have enjoyed a ball the night before as few were seen promenading down the walk. The sun marked our path with welcome warmth. 'Twas a fine day indeed. Trees had begun to bud—and the thought of them in full leaf sparked a thrill of hope within me. I believed Butterton to be in the heart of the countryside, where acres of trees and farmland waited like a fairyland. A sweet fantasy that Mr. Carter seemed determined to deny me.

The footman and Tessa walked ahead of me absently mumbling things I couldn't hear. I didn't mind. Felt good to look around me without being stared at and whispered about. I needed a moment alone to collect myself before speaking with Mr. Carter again.

As expected, he waited at the gate. His former coat had been changed to something finer, in a dark dove gray. He removed his matching hat and bowed, then lent me his arm. Very decent of him.

Shyness overtook me. I knew it was appropriate for him to offer assistance, and the expected response was to allow his genteel protection. Still, I hesitated a moment before placing my hand on his solid forearm.

We meandered along the path. I looked back at the footman and Tessa waiting nearby. A discussion of sorts occurred between them. Tessa's expression faltered. What were they saying? I stayed out of situations involving the servants. But as I'd never seen anything but a pleasant countenance from her, I knew something was amiss.

My heart beat quickly as I strode by Mr. Carter's side. The effect of touching a man's arm not belonging to Grandfather or one of my uncles, no doubt. Even if he was only exhibiting good manners. What did he intend to say? He led me to a bench, some distance away, down a short slope from my parents' grave. He planned to bring me to this exact spot.

He cleared his throat as we sat, tightly holding his gloves in his fist. His voice was quite serious, "Once again, I apologize for not being able to discuss matters with you sooner."

"Why me and not Grandfather?"

"Your grandfather isn't being asked to choose one of my cousins for a bridegroom."

Heat flared my cheeks. How did he know? Had he been listening in?

"I'm sorry that I must be forthright with you. Our time is short and there will be little time for private discussion on the way."

I nodded, my mouth gone dry. "What is your concern, sir?"

"Have you met the gentlemen in question? Any or all of them?"

"I have not." Nor any young man until Mr. Carter's arrival.

"Chinworth is my great uncle on my mother's side. He is a good man, and your grandfather had reason to trust him. His sons, however, are not."

The sliver of hope I clung to vanished beneath a sickening wave. Yet, how did he qualify his opinion? He could be lying. Why should I bow to his judgment? And why had he gone to all this trouble? "And you, sir, are trustworthy by comparison?"

His eyes flicked to mine in surprise. "I understand that we have little history between us, but in this, I ask that you consider carefully what I say."

"You mean to scare me away from your cousins." Little history? We had none.

"I mean to warn you. The frightening part for you would come if you married one of them."

"And you are an authority on whom I should marry?" Such a conversation to have with this not-altogether unattractive man.

"Miss Bartlett, I am sorry if my warning is off-putting. It isn't meant to be—or is it?" Amusement hung about his lips. Something about that look alarmed me.

"Your cousins are rogues?" I'd read about such scoundrels and even overheard gossip in the park on occasion. Entirely indecent. But never could a Chinworth be a cad.

He shook his head. "Greedy, yes. They help themselves to wine, women, and song, verily. They act as if they were owed such a reward. I would hate to see you join one of them in marriage. Treated like a possession. Your fortune would be laid to waste in a moment."

My fortune, once again a determination for my well-being. "I fear you speak slander." He seemed fearful as Grandfather concerning my wealth. But what did he have to do with who I chose as my future husband? He stood. "If only more women investigated the type of man they'd accepted *before* marriage took place..." He looked around the graveyard, his eyes had found it. My parents' gravestone. Clearly, he'd known where to look.

"You should communicate your concerns with Grandfather. He will decide if what you say has merit. It's not my place to challenge his wishes in this matter."

He shook his head. "And be booted from the door at the first negative word I say in Chinworth's direction? In all confidence, I risk enough by warning you alone." He draped his arm along the back of the bench. "Your grandfather does not question Chinworth, nor his sons. I could hardly contest him when my eyes and ears are the only proof I have to offer."

"You're correct, Grandfather wouldn't question him." So how did Mr. Carter dare to do so? Strange. Their own history must be deeply entwined. Else why attend to my future?

"Besides, my duty lies with you, Miss Bartlett. No one else."

His eyes held to mine with certainty. What did he mean? My heart sped. "Your duty?"

"Do you truly not know who I am?"

My patience wore a little thin. "The impertinent man who stalks me in the graveyard, who appears like a sudden shadow of late." I looked away at the empty tree branches that bounced with an eavesdropping squirrel.

He chuckled. "I'm sorry about that. I hadn't meant to startle you."

"Am I supposed to know who you are?" I was suddenly tired of the conversation.

"I wonder that your grandfather didn't tell you—or your uncles. But I suppose the topic is a painful one."

"You are all fearmongering and riddle-speaking!" I needed to return to Chatswick and finish packing. Enough of this.

"Come." He held his hand out to me, pulled me from the bench, and led me down the path to my parents' grave. The marble bowl of fruit, the vines, their names. He let go of my hand and pulled coins from his pocket and laid them there. His gentle touch showed that he cared.

"I don't understand."

His eyes drew mine, sharp and intense. "I knew your parents."

An unwelcome rush of jealousy surged. I had to look away. My life might have been so different had they lived. Perhaps I wouldn't be hidden among the hermits. I looked back at him, unexpected tears flanking my eyes. "How did you know them?" It seemed almost impossible to believe him.

"They lived not far from my family's estate."

"Go on." Suddenly I was intensely curious about what he'd next say.

"I was a mere lad of eleven. My father was sending me to Harrow for my first year of school away from home. Your mother and father were on their way to London to visit your grandfather and offered to take me along instead of my having to travel on the mail coach as planned." He looked at me and bowed his head. "You were two years old."

Whatever was he saying? "My parents died when I was two."

"Yes. In the carriage accident."

He hesitated to say more as I put the pieces together. "We – you and I – were on the carriage?"

He nodded. "We were." His hand made its way back to the marble stone. "We'd been suddenly chased into a ravine. When the carriage tipped you flung from your mother's arms, I caught you...barely." Emotion laced his voice. "Held on..." He swallowed and continued. "When I came awake, you were laying across my chest, sleeping. But I feared the worst, thought you dead. Thank the Lord you rallied and cried. We had survived, I know not how. The night was bright enough that I could see your father had died. Your mother nearly so."

My eyes and throat burned. I could almost see her in my mind.

"She begged me to take care of you—get you safely to London. I promised her I would."

He looked at me, his gaze questioning my memory. Hopeful. Not a flicker, nothing.

"We stayed with her until..."

"She died?"

"Yes. We climbed from the broken coach. I feared what I'd find—but the coachman was nowhere to be found. The coward. Not a sign of him." He paused. "Not long after, I realized that help wasn't coming. We were in the middle of nowhere and lost. And you, a mere babe. So, we walked down the road." A smile softly played about his lips. "Well, I walked. You had a free ride."

Such a wild tale, could it be true? Was there even a chance? Seeing emotion turn with his memory bade me to believe him.

"We came to an old coaching inn where the local magistrate was visiting. Well past midnight, mind you, when we arrived. Two children. I allowed them to think you were my sister. Indeed, the cook was anxious to take you from my arms, but I wouldn't let her. Not to mention the lock-hold you had around my neck."

"How did we get to London?"

He heaved a sigh. "When your mother and father were recovered, along with our things, the magistrate himself took us there. I carried you through the door of Chatswick and, it seems, you haven't left since."

All these years, Grandfather had allowed me to believe they'd died in a carriage accident and that was that. The end of my story. He never talked about them, never told me about their lives. Their portraits are nowhere to be seen. I'd even searched the attic and found nothing.

When I was sixteen, I'd pried from him where they were buried so that I could visit—and somehow feel closer to them. He bade the vicar show me. And so, I'd come alone each week since then.

"And if I ask, say, my uncles? They can corroborate your story?"

"Yes. They could. They were both there the day I brought you home."

"I see."

"They were overcome with grief as you can imagine."

"I am to conclude…" I couldn't speak. Everything grew muddy with the tragic story. I looked up at him needing more answers.

He picked up where I failed to ask. "My aforementioned duty to you comes honestly. By your mother's request, and by my promise to her before her death. I would take care of you, see you safely…"

"And by taking care of me, you mean to warn me from a wearisome future?" I shook my head. "I believe your duties were fulfilled when you left me with Grandfather." He had no further duty to me.

"Her voice plays in my memory—if only you could remember –no. It is well that you do not. She was desperate that I keep you safe." His solemnity gave me pause.

"If such a request incited so much devotion, why have you not visited? Ascertained my well-being years ago?" I'd been left to believe that no one outside of Chatswick's walls cared for me beyond my fortune. Was there truly someone else?

"You assume that I have not. Yes, I have visited on more than one occasion."

"I don't remember you, except recently." A silent witness to my life.

"Ah. You must understand that a boy's life and time are not his own. I was at Harrow for several years, and when not at school, at home—or in training. I couldn't come. When I did, I was not allowed entry."

"Hard to believe, given how congenial Grandfather and my uncles have been with you. At school with your father, who is an old friend? Why would they deny you?" And why did Grandfather introduce him to the family as though they'd never met?

"I don't know. Perhaps the memory torments him."

"Yet you are here now."

"At Chinworth's request."

Chinworth was the golden key, and it seemed that Grandfather would refuse that man nothing. "I'm not exactly sure what to do. Grandfather insists that I go. I cannot go against his wishes. Especially now."

He nodded. "I understand. But I am glad I've warned you. My cousins are attractive men. Convincing, cunning. When Chinworth told me his plan to bring you among them, I couldn't sit idly by watching."

"Because of an old promise." His honesty was refreshing.

"Because for a space of many hours and several miles of hard road, we suffered together, you and me. I'd never seen death before—and you were terrified. We were alone, weeping, clinging to each other. I didn't only promise your mother, I promised God." He shrugged his shoulders. "I don't know what His plans are for you, but I'm sure not going to sit by and watch the once darling little girl that clung to my neck be misused. Your heart must be protected. Nor will I allow my cousins to spoil the gift that the rest of your life is."

"A true hero, then." The words slipped off my tongue.

His eyes grew weary. "Please don't mock me."

My hand flung to my throat. "I did not mean to—I—please forgive me." I placed my hand on his sleeve. "If all that you say is true, then you saved my life. I thank you." The realization struck with greater ferocity as the seconds ticked by. Without him, I might have died. My mother's engraved name caught my eye. "You reassured my mother in her last moments. I am indebted to you." I always would be.

He tucked my hand back within the crook of his arm and led me away, down another pebbled path. "The story must be quite a shock."

Emotions clogged my throat. "You've carried the memory with you these many years."

"I cannot easily forget." His gaze searched mine. "I should have tried harder to help you. And sooner."

Help me sooner? With what? Only recently had I been made as an offering to Chinworth's sons. The generous choice I'd been given might be a lost cause. A wrong turn.

A cutting voice whispered through the hedge. I was being spied upon. "Is the lonely heiress affianced? Where did she meet him, I wonder? As trapped as the poor thing is?"

Mr. Carter tightened his hold and whispered in my ear. "Pay them no mind. Now. Or ever."

Chapter Four

I tossed and turned the night through. My trunks had been removed and loaded an hour before breakfast. I ate two bites of toast and swallowed some tea. Time for me to leave this room, my sanctuary.

My nerves grew again. My dreams had been rife with carriages pitching down ravines. I envisioned a deep cliff and a desperate boy surviving a shocking fate.

As far as I remembered, I'd never ridden in a carriage or any other sort of contraption. Except for the accident that reportedly claimed my parents' lives, that is. Grandfather didn't see the need to own anything beyond a small hack, which saw his secretary to and from various business engagements. He saw no need for me to travel except by foot.

The story of my rescue replayed in my mind. Facts presented themselves out of order, and questions dangled between them. The most glaring one of all: that my grandfather had not allowed Mr. Carter admittance until now. How very strange.

It was true, Grandfather had sent away more than one gentleman who'd attempted to call on me without proper introductions. Perhaps he'd forgotten who Mr. Carter belonged to, or what he'd done for me—and for the wife of his only son, my mother. But that didn't seem likely. Not when Grandfather and my uncles enjoyed a history of schooldays with Mr. Carter's father, recalling them with both detail and hilarity.

The freedom Grandfather had given Mr. Carter didn't match his earlier strictness concerning gentlemen. We'd been left alone on more than one occasion. Mr. Carter had been allowed to walk freely about Chatswick—no restrictions. He sat beside me on the settee last evening, and my uncles did not bat an eye. No. Their behavior and his story didn't add up.

Tessa opened my bedroom door. "Your grandfather would see you one last time."

Of course. I made my way to his bedside, and he pulled me into an embrace. "Dearest Emma. Write to me. And when you have made your choice," he winked, "do not delay in letting me know who the lucky fellow is. I shall try to wait patiently."

"I promise I will write." And that's all I would promise.

He released me. "Go now. Your carriage awaits." As though I were a princess on my way to destiny. Was I? Or maybe I was more like a commoner on the road to ruin!

I left his side and made my way to the foyer where Uncle Richard and Uncle Gerald gathered me into their arms in a gentle crush. Mr. Carter watched with some amusement as tears abounded between my uncles.

Uncle Gerald pulled a handkerchief from his coat pocket and blew his nose. "Take care of her. She is our most precious treasure." I remembered that I hadn't asked Uncle Gerald or

Richard to verify the carriage story. Was too late to do so now. I'd have to find another way to test the truth of the tale.

Mr. Carter bowed. "Always. I will see both Miss Bartlett and Miss Tessa safely to Butterton."

Uncle Richard handed Tessa a purse, and me one as well. "Mr. Carter carries sufficient funds to see you through to the end of summer." He winked. "Should you need more, you only need ask him."

The door shut behind me, the team of horses stamped the ground, anxious to be off. No sooner had the carriage door opened and shut behind me than I realized I had forgotten my chosen travel book. I jumped from my seat and raced back to the door.

Uncle Gerald's rich voice reverberated from the other side. "Thank goodness. She is finally gone."

What? I shrank back, stunned. Did they want me to leave so badly?

Tessa slipped her hand into mine and drew me back to the vehicle. "A case of nerves is to be expected."

"I thought I'd forgotten my book."

Tessa waved it before me. "I grabbed it on our way out. We haven't left a thing behind."

My nerves were playing tricks on me. I had misheard my uncles. Hadn't I?

Mr. Carter joined us and secured the door. "We have a good six hours of road ahead." The carriage jolted forward. "I've instructed the driver to stop halfway for refreshment. I expect we will arrive at Mayfield by late this afternoon if all goes well."

If all goes well... Not too likely, was it?

My mind once again returned to his story. Our story. The night's dreams replayed his words, visualizing what it must have been like. I could see my doting parents, a young version of Mr. Carter. Myself.

Nineteen years ago, we shared a carriage, a ride that ended tragically. I went rigid—and Tessa looped her arm around mine.

"It'll be alright, my lady."

Would it? A word arose from Mr. Carter's memory. We'd been *chased*. Suddenly chased—our coach fell down a ravine. We'd been *chased*.

Mr. Carter's eyes drew mine. He looked at me with some concern. Would that we were alone so I could ask him. What or who gave chase? Why? My questions multiplied.

He was a boy when the accident happened. Perhaps that part was a figment of his imagination. Perhaps all of it. I should give it neither credit nor worry over much.

Our coach moved faster, and my heart raced in time with the hooves. Too much change all at once. Too much...my nerves playing tricks on me again?

The sun struck like a sword through the window, directly upon my eyes in a blinding light. Mr. Carter lowered the shade and I blinked to recover. How odd to think that the light that causes sight, can also cause the opposite...

Mr. Carter reached within a leather pouch and pulled something out. The long barrel and handle, a trigger —a pistol?

I gasped. I'd only ever seen a sketch of such an item.

"Miss Bartlett, it is only a safety measure, quite common to carry them in coaches." He returned it to the hidden box. "In all probability, I won't have to use it." He cocked his head.

I swallowed down some fear. "Have you ever had to use one before?" My inexperience about the world overflowed yet again. I'd once thought it would be a wonderful place to explore, but now I wasn't so sure.

He paused and wove his hands together. "I am a weapons instructor, so I've had more practice than most people." His self-assurance calmed me.

That wasn't exactly what I'd asked though. Target practice was one thing, being in a dangerous situation was another.

Tessa consoled me yet again. "We are in as safe hands as possible."

I offered him a smile. "I don't doubt it."

Three hours passed in amicable silence. My spirit, however, was wound tight. We stopped at an inn for luncheon in a private parlor. Was a boon to stretch my legs after so long cramped in one place.

Tessa yawned. Perhaps she would sleep the remainder of the trip and I might ply Mr. Carter for more about the accident—and my parents. But he alighted a horse instead of climbing back inside with us. I wouldn't get the chance. At least not now. However, he would reside at Mayfield for the summer as well. Surely, I'd find a way to ask privately. A moment alone would be enough.

My thoughts turned back to Grandfather's reluctance to talk about Mother and Father. I so wished he had portraits of them.

A sudden longing rose within me to feel their arms about me as I had my uncles. To remember their love. Had they loved me like these old men claimed to?

It was I who fell asleep soon after we'd departed the inn. I hardly know when I dropped off. We'd passed through a few appealing villages until the landscape changed, and then the countryside. The rolling and jolting of the carriage lulled me to sleep.

Tessa patted my cheek. "My lady, we are almost there."

I looked out of the window as we drew into Mayfield. Such a large, rambling estate compared to home. It engulfed the land it stood upon, with great yawning windows. My heart pounded. Why had I allowed myself to be pushed to come? This was a mistake. I resisted the urge to beg the driver to turn around—and by all means, take me back to the only life I knew. The only one that was safe.

Tessa reached about me. "Here, let me affix your bonnet. There now. Mussed hair is properly hidden." Tessa winked. "I'll be right beside you, dear."

"I thank you."

"And don't forget, I pray for you."

I nodded. Her words were an anchor.

The door opened and Mr. Carter appeared to help me down the steps. In a low voice, he reminded me. "Don't forget what I told you."

That would be impossible. I disembarked and before me stood three tall, handsome gentlemen with raven black hair, an older silvered gentleman who must be Chinworth, and beside him, a slip of a girl with the palest blonde hair I'd ever seen. Such striking contrast. Whoever was she?

The girl curtsied, the others bowed in unison. The older man stepped forward. "You are most welcome here, Miss Bartlett! How we have longed to make your acquaintance!" He nodded to Mr. Carter. "Thank you, Joseph."

I curtsied as a troop of goliath-sized dogs – heavy, enormous ones – bounded through the doorway and leaped upon me. Such manners!

Chapter Five

Two of the gentlemen roared amid my scream, another barely stifled his laughter—someone else, I'm not sure who, called them off as Mr. Carter blocked me from the enormous creatures. I would not call this a particularly positive first impression.

Footmen and servants grabbed them by the collars and thankfully took the wild beasts away as I attempted to calm myself.

Chinworth sputtered. "Miss Bartlett—please accept our abject apology. Ezra was supposed to lock them up. He will be reprimanded, you may be sure." He peered at me closely, inspecting.

I tried not to shrink under his perusal...

"None of them bit you, did they? They are still puppies, mind you. Big as they are."

Puppies? I shook my head, nerves welled up, threatening to spill over into tears. Struggled to keep my anxiety in check.

One of the younger men stepped forward and bowed. "Zachary, at your service." He offered his arm. "Do come in and take some tea. You must be weary from your journey."

His refined voice seemed self-possessed. In complete control. So unlike Uncle Richard who would simply declare: tea! With that jolly grin of his. And then we would have it. This formality gave me pause. I'd been too much at home and too comfortable in my isolation from proper society.

We sat in the grand drawing room, minus the young girl who dashed away as soon as we entered the foyer. The housekeeper sat knitting at the other end of the room, half hidden by a large hunting tapestry. For propriety's sake. I was glad for her presence as Tessa was upstairs putting away our things. Mr. Carter had also disappeared. How I wished he had not.

For fifteen minutes, I was at the mercy of what Grandfather considered my fate and what Mr. Carter considered a fearsome folly.

I looked about the room that was so well appointed one would never guess that Mayfield lacked a mistress. Gilded framed artwork lined the walls, the marble mantelpiece shone, and the chairs, I couldn't help but notice, sported claw feet digging sharp nails into the knotted wool rug

The three young men sat in a row and Mr. Chinworth joined me on the settee. The jury was watching. I cradled my teacup noticing each nervous rattle. Was all I could do to draw tea between my lips without shaking. Between these men and the dogs, I was undone. Still, I kept up a hopeful aspect.

"How is Bartlett? Truly, we were expecting him to arrive with you."

"He sends his deepest regrets. An unfortunate attack of the gout keeps him to his bed." I pulled the letter he'd sent along from my reticule. "He very much desired to see you again."

Chinworth accepted the letter. "And I him! By golly, it's been too many years. And here is his lovely granddaughter in my own home. Will Mayfield be a happy escape for you, do you think?"

The brothers shifted in their chairs, one of them smirked.

"I daresay it will be delightful to spend the warm months ahead in such a beautiful place."

"If not a tad boring." One of them said, but I didn't catch who.

"Nonsense." Chinworth's voice clipped.

Clearly, one of the brothers wasn't terribly pleased I'd come. Did they know the purpose? Likely. I raised the teacup again and found myself calmer this time.

Chinworth pointed with his hand to his sons. "Zachary has introduced himself, but here is Samuel, my oldest..." his shoulders were broader than Zachary's, his forehead lower. "And this is Tobias." Tobias bowed. His chin jutted out, and his hair curled unlike the other two.

"If I had known old Bartlett had such a beauty of a granddaughter, I would have sent for you sooner!"

A blush crept up my neck. Was his observation honest? I didn't know if I was truly beautiful, but I did know that my inheritance made me attractive to many. This, I shrank from. Though I tried to hide my discomfort as best as I could. Moments later, the uncomfortable reception blessedly over, the housekeeper at last led me up the grand staircase.

I decided then and there that I would get through these months and perhaps, go home earlier than expected. I hoped my choice to do so would be mine alone. The young Chinworth's passive reception made this an easy decision, regardless of Mr. Carter's warning. Perhaps he need not be concerned. Those boys appeared to have little interest in my acquaintance.

How many weeks should I wait until I make the request to leave? What was an appropriate time frame? I followed the old woman down the large hall, hardly noticing the direction she led me. Six weeks ought to resolve any curiosity they had about me.

I wanted to marry for love. Not because of my inheritance. Would that God make it possible. Another plea to add to Tessa's prayers, if I dared tell her.

The housekeeper opened the door and stood back so that I could walk in first. I glanced at her welcome smile. Her salt and pepper hair drew tightly back from a face that was more pleasing than I first thought. In fact, she beamed.

"Mr. Chinworth had these rooms redone for your arrival, my lady. I hope you approve."

Was this done only out of kindness? "How can I not?" Indeed, the walls were coated in the palest cream. I turned to see that a series of four square, side-by-side windows faced a large lake, glistening in the sunset. It curved with the land as far as the eye could see.

The fabrics were in delicate shades of green as though summer had prematurely bloomed. I'd never been in a more beautiful space.

Had the rooms been redone for my arrival alone? My fortune must be terribly important to them to go through the trouble.

"And your personal maid is in the room next door, on the other side of your private parlor." She opened yet another door to reveal a larger room in the same coloring, only with a splash of lavender here and there. A fire snapped in the grate and primroses graced vases on the mantelpiece.

"Very lovely." It was. Perhaps I could find refuge here.

"His lordship will be happy to hear that you approve." She showed me quaintly embroidered bell pulls. "Don't hesitate to ring so that we may make your stay as comfortable as possible."

I nodded. I had no words.

"My master assumes that since you had a long journey, perhaps you would enjoy supper in your rooms tonight? It will be delivered in two hours. Should you like a bath to be drawn?"

"Very much so, thank you. I should like my maid to dine with me tonight, as I have things to discuss with her."

She nodded. My odd request didn't surprise her. Perhaps she understood how alone I was in this new, strange place. Until today's travels and our brief repast at the inn, I had never dined with Tessa. Why was that so?

Tessa opened the door of her apartment, curtsied, and stood beside the fireplace.

"Very well then," the housekeeper curtsied as well. "You may call me Johnson." She nodded to Tessa. "Tessa will show you to the breakfast room in the morning. Good evening."

And that was that. With little pomp, a new phase in my existence had begun.

Later, as we dined upon a rich meal of creamy chicken, cold fruit, cheese, and salad greens, a patter of feet sounded outside of my door. Not those dogs again! Snuffling, a growl, then a paw scratched. Another animal joined the efforts, its smaller paw shoved into the gap.

Tessa giggled. "The scent of food has drawn the dogs to your door."

I whispered. "Aren't you afraid?"

"Why, no. Of course not."

"But they attacked me."

"Pardon me, my lady, but that was no attack. They were merely introducing themselves. A bit wild-like, mind you."

"Had they been taught to bow like gentlemen, I might not have screamed." I lowered my fork. "Will they jump on me again?"

"I hope not, my lady. But if they do, push them down and tell them no. Let them see your strength."

"Simply tell them no?" At least the beasts were on the other side of the door as I contemplated such defiance.

Tessa nodded. "I'll not let you get hurt."

It didn't help that I feared both man and beast in this house. As it stood, the dogs would do the prowling, and the gentlemen's disinterest would make leaving all the easier.

I slept restlessly again, ever mindful that I wasn't snuggled against my own pillows and mattress and that enormous dogs roamed these halls. Again, I was grateful for my own room.

Moonlight slipped through the window making the shadows play upon the wall. I climbed from bed, pulled back the drapes, and set my gaze upon the silvered lake as thin, black clouds floated over the moon like a mourning veil taken by a breeze.

Did Grandfather rest easy knowing I wasn't there? I missed him.

And was Mr. Carter right about his cousins? How could I know for sure?

For the first time in my life, I realized that I needed to make plans for what might happen when this venture completed. I intended to take my life into my own hands, inheritance or not. I would not let my fortune define – or confine – me. For years, I'd gone along with my quiet, day-to-day doings, waiting for something good or interesting to happen. And while my present situation was no doubt diverting, I knew it wouldn't sustain me. I needed something more to live for other than being an heiress.

Truly, something worth living and dying for.

Mr. Carter's words came back to me. *"I'm sure not going to sit by and watch the once darling little girl that clung to my neck be misused. Nor will I allow my cousins to spoil the gift that the rest of your life is."* The man seemed to care about me.

He'd said that my life was a gift. To myself? To others? Either way, I knew with a profound surge of wakefulness that I mustn't let it be spoiled. No matter who, no matter what. God wouldn't want me to waste my inheritance.

I'd survived without knowing my own story. I'd been preserved and rescued. Only now did I know the truth.

I clutched my robe as my newfound strength parried with fear. I didn't know what I was going to do or how. An unattached woman of some education, I laughed, with few means of my own. Entirely untried by society. What good could I possibly be – or do – anywhere? *Remember*, I told myself. *Remember that my life is a gift...Why did you let me live, God?*

I gazed across the lake again, its unknown depths akin to my future. I basked in the moment and prayed a few stumbling prayers. Did it matter to God that I used my own words instead of repeating His? I begged His forgiveness just in case. My former restlessness shifted to something near peace. A peace I desperately desired to cling to.

I lifted my finger to touch the moon behind the glass, but something caught my eye. Two dark figures moved about the edge of the water—then disappeared. Another stealthy form trailed some distance behind them, then also disappeared.

Nighttime is when much wretchedness happens, Grandfather had been known to say. So, we never went anywhere after dark. I cringed and closed the draperies, glad those men, whoever they were, weren't close to Mayfield. I thought being this far from London meant I'd be safe from such dark doings. Unless they were only innocents on a midnight stroll? Seemed unlikely.

I crawled back into bed and snuggled beneath the blankets. Perhaps fishermen were out and about catching our breakfast.

Didn't people do that in the countryside? Must be. Nay, surely I wouldn't find wretchedness happening in such idyllic surroundings, despite the supposed roguish natures of the Chinworth gentlemen. I needed hard evidence before making up my mind.

CHAPTER SIX

Tessa took her time with my hair this morning—she arranged a new style, a departure from twists along the sides swept up into a spiral. Rather this time, she pulled generous curls to trail down the back of my neck, with two prominent ringlets in front. Definitely flattering.

"There now. Let your beauty shine." She winked into the mirror.

"I'm not sure it's right for me to stay here." I bit my lip. "I know very well that I won't choose or accept any of the Chinworth gentlemen." How could I?

"I'm sure you are a good judge of character. But who knows? One of them may be found worthy of your attention." She tucked a final pin into my hair. "Give it more time."

Tessa didn't know what Mr. Carter had told me. This, I kept close to my vest. The last thing I needed was gossip to begin below stairs, the kind that might work its way to the ears of my host. That would be ghastly for all involved.

She smiled. "They are very handsome, wouldn't you say?"

Um...I would not say. "I don't take a fancy to them. Not nearly, not in the least. I trespass upon Mayfield, with no hope for our families' union. I would feel a thief, in a way."

"Nonsense." She placed her hands on her hips. "You aren't a thief, but you are very lovely indeed." She motioned for the door. "Time for breakfast. Put on your best expression."

Which meant, time to face the bevy of gentlemen again. Would I have the pleasure of the young woman's company? Was she their sister? I laughed at the irony. My home had ever been in the company of aged bachelors. Again, I found myself surrounded by men. If only my time could be balanced by young ladies of my own age.

When Mrs. Grayson left, I lost my only true friend. I'd grieved for an entire year before accepting her departure. And with that thought, I determined to write —it had been a few months. I knew that she traveled to Italy with her charge's family, but even so, sharing my thoughts with her might ease my burden.

I brushed a hand down my skirt as Tessa opened the door. "Follow me, dear." She led the way. I confess I watched for the wolfhounds and the little terrier. I feared they would bound from behind a settee and devour me whole for breakfast.

"The dogs have been put away, my lady, if that's what you're worried about."

"Does it show? I am relieved." A nervous laugh escaped my throat.

Down the steps I went, then another short hall, and into a more cheerful room I'd never seen before. Fresh-cut roses dripped from an etched silver vase in the center of a large, round table dressed in a white cloth. A buffet filled with all manner of food stood waiting. I'd entered alone, but a moment later in came the gentlemen.

My breathing hitched and my stays seemed tighter than usual.

Mr. Chinworth bowed, "Good morning, I trust you rested well?"

"Indeed, sir." When I finally fell asleep after my revolutionary thoughts.

Samuel, Zachary, and Tobias bowed as well, and the oldest, Samuel, seated me with great care and attention.

Mr. Carter walked in. "Forgive me, I am late." He smiled and bowed. "Good morning, Miss Bartlett."

I nodded. "Mr. Carter." I turned to Mr. Chinworth, all too aware of so much masculinity in one small room. "Do you not have a daughter?"

He picked up his plate and approached the buffet. "Ah, you mean Cecily. Yes." He dumped a sausage on his plate. "She has a delicate constitution and usually rises after luncheon." On went a scoop of eggs, slices of bread. "She is most anxious to spend time with you."

Tobias laughed. "Look around the room, Father. I daresay our guest might feel more at home with additional female company."

"Oh?" Mr. Chinworth looked concerned as he took his seat next to me.

"It is of no consequence." Was that a lie? "Indeed, I've spent these many years with naught but Grandfather and my uncles.

I am quite accustomed to the presence of well-behaved elder gentlemen." Just not the other kind – young and seeking a spouse. How long would it take to grow accustomed to these handsome, foreboding men? I smiled and made my way to the buffet pretending a great interest in the eggs and fish before me.

Mr. Carter joined me. I felt more at ease with him in the room. I believed, or rather hoped, that if I did need to leave for some reason, Mr. Carter wouldn't hesitate to help me return home.

"Do tell me," I put on the most social voice I could muster. "Is the lake good for fishing?"

Mr. Carter looked at me in surprise, as did the rest of the men.

Mr. Chinworth smiled. "Does the lady enjoy fishing? You are a rare sort."

"Oh, I've never attempted it. I don't know if I would enjoy the process or not. I thought perhaps we might be eating last night's catch." The small piece of fried fish on my plate begged what I'd seen to be true.

Samuel's brows rose. "Last night's catch?"

"Didn't I see men fishing about the lake last night?"

Mr. Chinworth sat in silence. Tobias laughed low. Samuel nodded his head slowly as glances were shared. "Why yes, Miss Bartlett, I believe you did see a few fellows hard at work last night."

Zachary joined in. "Our lake is known for offering up a decent night's catch. Assuming you work hard enough."

Tobias's laugh grew, then silenced when Mr. Chinworth raised his hand. Had they been trodding upon an unseen line?

A family secret of sorts? "I propose that one of you take our honored guest to the lake and see if she can be persuaded to like fishing. Any volunteers?"

I acquiesced. "Sounds...lovely." Me, the honored guest. I wanted to laugh behind my napkin. If I weren't the heiress, I'm pretty sure I wouldn't be so exalted. No. Nothing about this bespoke of care or mutual respect. After last night's praying, my choices were becoming clearer. I wasn't choosing these men, but truths instead. They would serve me and my heart better. I would hold fast to them and be so guided.

Truth: my grandfather wants me to be properly joined to someone who can care for me on a level I am well accustomed to. A more worthy truth: I am not money and cannot be properly affianced to anyone who cares more about money than me.

Mr. Chinworth interrupted my musing. "Meanwhile, I believe Zachary is to give you a tour of the house at ten o'clock." He counted with his fingers. "Luncheon will be at noon, tea at four, supper at eight. I hope that suits?"

Sounded like a full schedule. And a very filling one at that. It seemed my day would revolve around exact mealtimes. "Of course." I wondered about the dogs. "I have one question. Will the dogs be..."

A bark answered my query. I started.

"Ah. Joseph? Will you do the honor of properly introducing Miss Bartlett to the dogs this morning?"

"I'd be happy to."

"I believe I well-met them yesterday."

Tobias laughed outright this time. "Which is why Father must insist that you get to know them. Next time you meet, they will not leap." He held up his hand. "You need to learn how to stop them if you're going to summer here. We have no intention of keeping them penned up all day. They wouldn't have it."

Mr. Chinworth nodded. "Quite right."

I was surrounded. By gentlemen and dogs alike. Which would be the kinder set?

At the end of breakfast, everyone scattered away from me except Mr. Carter, who pulled my chair. At last, we were alone.

"Ready to be reacquainted with the animals? Perhaps they'll become your best companions here."

"I'm not so sure."

"Not to worry," he smiled. "They are gentle enough – unless the cook accidentally leaves the chicken coop open. It's happened before. Feathers everywhere."

He led me down a narrow hall that went past the cavernous kitchens. The back door led to a site not seen from any of the windows on the formal side of the estate. Here were gardens being readied for planting, a glass house for growing winter vegetables, and a stone path leading to the stables.

A cottage nestled by a low hill not far from us. The gamekeeper's abode, I presumed, with smoke curling from the chimney and bright red curtains fluttering at one open window. Baking bread scented the air and begged me to cross the threshold. How I dearly wished to peek inside.

Was like something I'd read from storybooks as a child. Complete with a mother, father, and a kind old grandfather who sat with children upon his knee in front of a cozy fire. With enthusiasm, he would regale them with stories of his own childhood.

The old yearning pulled. I wanted to be settled in such a home. My soul tugged until it hurt.

Did the fireplace boast a steaming copper kettle, ready for tea-making? Were pickles in the crockery, apples in a barrel, and simple potato and cream suppers in a bowl? Did the family that circled the table sing songs of an evening? I'd always wanted to do so. That and run barefoot like a poor shepherdess on the hillside, surrounded by sheep. What would Grandfather think of my wild thoughts?

I needed to stop the fantasy. "Who lives in that cottage?"

"Ah, that would be Mr. Greenwood and his wife. He is the gamekeeper here."

As I thought.

"Do they have children?"

"William and Michael serve in the army, and the young twins—Josie and Timothy are at school."

"Far from home?"

"No indeed. Just down the road in Butterton."

The air had warmed since yesterday, even the breeze held hints of summer. I'd discard my shawl soon. "Would you have liked to be educated within your village instead of Harrow?"

Mr. Carter paused. "That's a hard question. I should have preferred to stay home, near my own parents. But since Father had attended Harrow, and his father before him, you might say it was my destiny."

"Are we destined to certain times and places? Have we no choice in the matter?" My moon-watching had set in motion so many restless thoughts, I could scarcely stop them.

He paused and held his hand out to me. "All I know is that if I hadn't been on my way to Harrow, with your parents on that coach, you might not have survived." I gave him my hand as he led me over a steep stile. "God made sure someone was there to catch you. Care for you."

I bounced to the ground and he reached out to steady me, then placed my hand in the fold of his arm.

I needed to make the most of our time alone. Would I have another chance? "I have more questions about what happened that night." I looked him in the eye.

His jaw tightened, yet his eyes filled with compassion. "I believe I told you all there is to know. But I'll answer any question you have."

I gulped. "You said we'd been chased off the road and into a steep ravine. What about the driver? You never said what happened to him. I can't get the whole horrible picture out of my mind."

"Ah. I understand." His lips pursed before he looked up to the spotty clouds littering a light blue sky. We turned the corner past the stables and stopped in a lean-to shed. Thankfully, the dogs were nowhere to be seen.

"So, there is more to the story?" My heart sped.

He released me, then leaned against a rough, wooden beam and folded his arms. "Happened so long ago, it's hardly relevant now."

He didn't want me to know. Or worry... Why? "I grew up without parents because of that accident." Hurt filled my voice. "And I'm finally finding out about your part in my story."

"The facts aren't going to help you, Miss Bartlett." His brown eyes exuded pity.

"I would still know. Please, Mr. Carter," This gaping hole needed to be filled, no matter how difficult.

"Alright. I warn you, there isn't much to tell." He looked into the distance, his memory stirring. "We were already traveling at a good pace but sped up. Trying to outrun them. I can still hear the coachman's whip crack the air. Angry shouting, the coachman, I guess."

"I looked through the back window and saw two riders racing towards us. A gun fired. Your father looked outside, shouted at the driver — thumped the ceiling with his walking stick. You began to wail. The carriage sped on. Another shot fired—and down we went. Tumbling, crashing. You know the rest of the story."

Two riders... "Highwaymen?"

"As the magistrate presumed." His face spoke volumes.

"But you didn't think so?"

"Miss Bartlett, nothing was taken from the carriage after we escaped."

"Nothing?"

"Not even your mother's diamonds."

My mother had diamonds? I didn't know. Had Grandfather kept any of her belongings? Or Father's? "What happened to the driver? Was he ever found?"

"That part remains a mystery. His whereabouts were never discovered."

"So strange. That highwaymen would take nothing..."

"Exactly what I told the magistrate in a letter."

"What did he say?"

"He refused to listen to a mere boy, no matter whose son I was." He glanced around the corner of the building. "I wrote multiple times until the man could stand me no longer. He threatened to punish me if I continued to inquire about the closed investigation."

"Did that stop you?"

He quirked a smile. "No. Of course not."

"Were you punished as threatened?"

"I was." I covered my mouth with my hand as the story flowed from his lips. He hadn't stopped searching for answers.

"I was but sixteen years old at my last inquiry. Riding my horse on holiday at Wyndhouse. Strangers approached on faster steeds. They yanked me off the saddle and I was beaten bloody, my last letter to the magistrate stuffed into my mouth." He looked away from me. "Ink isn't so tasty."

"Mr. Carter." A fury ran through my bones. "How could this happen?"

He shook his head. "There is great evil in this world."

"Did you tell your father?"

"Didn't have to. Hiding my wounds would have been impossible." Mr. Carter rubbed his knuckles. "My father did what any decent man would do for his son. He taught me to fight.

Defend myself. This is why I do what I do—and why I'm going to help Lord Banbury's heir, Matthew, get on his feet again."

Yet another intrigue I didn't know or understand. More questions. Always more.

"Call it fate or destiny, what happened to me has informed my entire life. My very future. And if I now have opportunities to help others as a result of my own anguish. I'm not the least bit sorry."

"Well, I am. You were only sixteen years of age! Children should never suffer as you have."

"Sixteen is hardly a child." He lifted his hand to my cheek and swiped away the rogue tear slipping from my eye. "God knows that suffering produces perseverance. My wounds have long healed, Miss Bartlett."

"The scar, by your ear?" I examined it again.

He lifted his hand to the jagged place. "From the carriage accident."

"After all that you never found out who chased my parents to their deaths? And what of this magistrate who did you great ill?"

He inclined his head at the sound of snorting creatures. "I think the dogs are coming."

The wolf hounds bounded around the corner and my knees buckled.

I looked at Mr. Carter, hoping for an offer of his arm.

CHAPTER SEVEN

His strong arms kept me from sinking to the ground as fear snaked tight around my middle.

"Do not worry, Miss Bartlett. As I said, they are gentle beasts."

The wolf hounds ran like a herd of untamed horses toward me and I trembled. From the terrible story and the overeager dogs.

"Gently, now."

The dogs slowed as they approached us, as large as ponies, covered in slate gray fur. His hands remained about my shoulders. I must seem a foolish female, growing faint at the first sign of the family pets. Were they simply being friendly?

Mr. Carter released me, put a hand flat before them. "Sit."

The group, I counted four, sat like soldiers under command.

"Take off your glove so you can introduce yourself."

Was he serious? "Am I to shake hands?" Indeed, my hands already shook.

"In a manner of speaking." They need to get to know your scent.

I pulled my glove off and Mr. Carter took my bare hand in his, my breath catching at the warmth of his touch. I had to trust this man. Wanted to.

"Here." He guided my hand to the nose of the first dog who gave it a long sniff. He wouldn't bite me. Cast that thought from my mind. The hound seemed satisfied as we moved to the next dog, then the next. The last gave me an unexpected lick as I tensed.

"See? The pitiful animals want to get to know you. That's all." His encouraging face almost convinced me.

A little terrier bounded in the midst of them and took my dress hem between his teeth. "Oh!" The beast would ruin it.

"Off, Pascal."

Pascal sat at the same hand motion Mr. Carter had used with the others.

"Now this one is a handful, but she's a good dog. Needs someone to play with her." He scratched her behind the ears.

A bell rang and the dogs began to whine. A canine chorus.

"It's their mealtime." Mr. Carter clapped his hands and they bounded away.

"Will they obey me as they have done you?"

"With time I would certainly hope so. You are in charge, Miss Bartlett. Not them. Make sure they know who is boss, and you shouldn't have any further problems."

I was skeptical. Sounded far too easy.

Zachary made his way towards us, his imposing figure blocking the sun. Time for my tour of the house.

Mr. Carter laughed low. "You might employ the same tactics with my dear cousins. Make sure they know *you're* in charge. Not them."

"I believe I can safely say that they show little to no interest in me, which should no doubt relieve your mind."

"I beg you still be wary."

Zachary showed me his perfect row of teeth. "I hope you had a better meeting this time around?"

"I did, thank you." No help from him.

"Shall we?" He offered his arm, then spoke to Mr. Carter. "Cross swords at two? In the ballroom?"

Mr. Carter smiled. "Prepared to be beaten again, are you? Very well. It will be my pleasure." He bowed. "Enjoy your tour, Miss Bartlett."

I wasn't sure I could, not with those two questions still burning in my mind. Trouble had come to him for trying to find out what caused our deadly encounter all those years ago. Would danger be directed at me if I sought an answer as well? My social rank would lend greater weight, but as a woman, and without Grandfather's knowledge and support, would I even be able to proceed? I couldn't blame Mr. Carter for dropping the matter. As he'd said, it happened long ago.

Magistrates were supposed to be upstanding men, not bullies. Zachary led me away, but I turned back, hopeful. Mr. Carter's eyes caught mine and held them.

And in that mere moment, my heart was captured by the boy who had suffered for the truth. And the man he'd become. My sad history may not be relevant today, but his sacrifice surely was.

We ventured a circle around the estate first and the farther we walked away from the stables, the more I felt the distance between Mr. Carter and me. I'd only known him for a few days. Yet I felt bound by our story. I couldn't explain it with logic. The separation chafed. I wanted to see him, hear his voice.

I hoped we'd be able to talk again soon—and perhaps, once my curiosity was satisfied, I could move onward without feeling the prickly sting of Grandfather's secrets. Withholding the truth had done its damage no matter how well-intentioned their efforts to protect me.

"How do you like it?" Zachary interrupted my thoughts. He held his hand towards an intriguing folly, hidden within a high thicket of trees that arched over a dome held aloft by thick Grecian columns. "Come."

He guided me towards a marble Grecian lady dancing within the center, a bunch of grapes dangling from one hand. She danced to an unheard tune, celebrating, yet unsmiling. The old adage arose: *Eat, drink, and be merry, for tomorrow we die...*

Warnings flitted through my mind. "Perhaps I should request Tessa to join us." To be in such a secluded place alone with a man bespoke of scandal. Never mind that I'd been in a private corner with Mr. Carter – and no one else. Hadn't even thought of the implications of that. "Nonsense." He rose to his toes, searching. "The little scamp thinks she can hide from me," His voice rose, "I will find her if she doesn't show herself this instant! Repercussions shall ensue!" He forced a smile.

A squeal rent the air as the slender blonde-haired child dashed from behind the structure. She saw me and paused before dipping into a low curtsy.

Zachary's brows rose. "Run from Nurse again, did you?"

She shrugged as her words bit the air, "The medicine doesn't help, I cannot abide it."

"Well then, I won't reveal your hiding place in the folly for at least an hour. But you must go back by luncheon, or you-know-who will come knocking."

"May I stay here with you and Miss Bartlett?" Her round blue eyes begged.

Zachary nodded. "So you shall play chaperone. How utterly delightful." His attitude and tone had both altered.

She approached me. "I'm Cecily, Miss Bartlett. In case no one told you." She curtsied again, her smile bright.

"I'm pleased to make your acquaintance, Miss Chinworth."

"Have you chosen one of my brothers yet?" How delightfully blunt.

Her frank question shocked and my face burned with embarrassment.

Zachary started for her, but she ran from his grasp. "Get back to Nurse, you little imp!" He turned back to me, flashing a broad smile. "Do forgive her, she hasn't many diversions, you know."

This I could understand. Her mischievous nature needed a firm governess' hand. And perhaps a circle of friends.

"If I may be so bold to ask? What ails her?"

"Cecily was born too early. Her arrival killed our mother."

Such harsh words to hang upon an innocent child.

"She has seizures occasionally. We can neither account for them nor cure them." He was matter-of-fact.

"I am sorry to hear it."

"Oh don't feel too sorry for her. She is spoiled beyond compare and though she'll probably die young, she'll have enjoyed every luxury." He blew an impatient breath. "Father has seen to that."

His coldness slipped like ice down my spine. I shivered and pulled my shawl more tightly about me. He didn't display even an ounce of sympathy for the child.

"I believe we should go inside where it's warmer and finish our tour there." I placed my hand in the crook of his arm again. "How should you like to see a library of nearly four hundred volumes?"

"Only four hundred?" I was sure Grandfather's library boasted more.

"Are you a great reader, Miss Bartlett?"

I smiled. "Most certainly." Though I enjoyed books immensely, I longed to live a real story. One with an enchanting ending.

We entered the front doors. Tessa waited for me and I was grateful for her presence.

Room by room, the estate bore a refined opulence. Tessa trailed behind us as Zachary pointed out this room and that space. He seemed rushed and had lost his relaxed manner when we stepped back inside. Any potential interest in me as a spouse seemed to have disappeared.

Zachary took the lead down a narrow hall. Voices rumbled, the edge of a coat seen through a nearby doorway.

Overheard were the words: "You *will* escort her to the Sherborne's, Friday next."

The responding voice was tight with fury. "Alright. As if I have a choice."

Zachary backed up. "Seems I've taken you in the wrong direction. My apologies. I meant to lead us to the solarium."

"Indeed." I glanced at Tessa as the low boom of voices died down. We must have been near Mr. Chinworth's study. I could only guess that the gentleman speaking was one of Zachary's brothers: Samuel or Tobias. One thing was clear, that individual didn't want to escort me. But was being forced to. If only I could put them all out of their misery and tell them immediately that I did not seek their suits. Didn't want them. Could I say the words even now?

Without heed for propriety, Mr. Chinworth pronounced loud and clear, "She is an heiress, you ninny. Nothing else matters."

Silence fell. Hadn't the sons already learned this crucial fact about me? No wonder the initial disinterest.

Clearly, Zachary had overheard as well. He hurried us around the corner then paused his steps and inclined his head. He turned slowly and offered his arm. "Forgive me, I haven't been attentive to the time, Miss Bartlett. Let me escort you to luncheon." He didn't acknowledge the awkwardness of the situation.

The platter of cold cheeses and meats contrasted noticeably with the now much warmer regards I was receiving from the gentlemen. My, such attention! Such honor! The strong reminders from Mr. Chinworth triggered a reconsideration of my presence. Felt a bit queasy at their new interest.

Mr. Carter was not there to witness the phony flirtations. How I wish he had been.

I'm certain we would have shared a knowing glance and secret smile at their insincerity.

CHAPTER EIGHT

Two days passed before gaining another scrap of time with Mr. Carter. The Chinworth brothers had taken me in hand earnestly after discovering my financial status. All except the oldest—Samuel. He performed his duties well while his father watched, but as soon as Mr. Chinworth left the room, he became distant once more. Not that I minded.

Perhaps there was one Chinworth brother not stalking my wealth. Yet neither did he seem to care for me one whit. Indeed, his frown deepened each day and the glances from Zachary and Tobias furthered his angst, and heightened their humor. It was in such a moment that Samuel requested to speak to them privately, leaving Tessa and me alone in the drawing room after supper.

Mr. Carter walked in after they had gone. Tessa was intent upon her needlework in the late sun streaming in through the window. Mr. Carter took the seat opposite.

"How goes the courting?"

I appreciated the irony. "Would you believe they didn't know of my inheritance until after I arrived?"

He frowned. "Is that so?"

"Tis a strange thing to overhear my host prod his son into escorting me to some fancy affair, then sweeten the deal with that knowledge. Since then, Zachary and Tobias have been vying for a seat beside me." I shrugged. "Samuel does not care to compete."

Mr. Carter fiddled with a loose button. "I wouldn't be so sure."

"Why do you say that?"

"If there's anything Samuel cares about more than his own life, it's money."

"Oh." And by way of money, me.

Mr. Chinworth's form filled the doorway, his normally smiling face frowned. He held a letter in his hands. His sons filed in behind him, a tall, somber wave of handsome gentlemen I wouldn't choose even if I were penniless.

"My dear." Mr. Chinworth held his hand out. "Something has happened."

Mr. Carter stood. "What is it, Uncle?"

"I am so sorry to be the bearer of bad news." He frowned and his brows rose with concern. "Your grandfather took a turn for the worse." He placed a hand over his heart. "My dear old friend..."

I stood, ready to fly back to London. "I must go to him this instant."

Mr. Chinworth shook his head. "No, my dear. It is too late already. He is dead, Miss Bartlett. I am so sorry."

Dead? No. I could not comprehend this.

Strong hands guided me to my seat. Only weeks ago, I had jokingly thought about having my fortune at my own disposal. Grandfather would be gone, if that were the case. Guilt surged as my heart broke. I hadn't wanted his death. Not that. Never. *No...*

A handkerchief was pressed into my hands.

Mr. Chinworth's voice rang, "Wine for the girl, she's had a shock."

I didn't want wine. "I need to go back to London. My uncles, they will need me." Uncle Richard and Uncle Gerald must be heartbroken. This I knew for certain.

"There, there." Mr. Chinworth sat beside me. "Take this wine, and Tessa will see you to your room. "We'll talk tomorrow."

Yes. Tomorrow. I swallowed the sweet wine that left a burning trail down my throat. I rarely drank it, why did I now? I wasn't thinking clearly. The room grew fuzzy. I tried to stand but floated instead. Hands steadied me, voices sounded as though from another room.

"What did you give her, Uncle?" Mr. Carter seemed concerned.

"A good night's rest..."

"You had no right..."

That was the last I remember. What was happening? I felt a jostle, a crunch, arms about me. *Mr. Carter?* I tried to call for him, but he was far, far away.

I knew nothing until morning. Or was it afternoon? How long had I slept? My tongue stuck to the roof of my mouth, and my throat was so very dry. My head as thick as a London fog.

I blinked awake slowly, trying to place where I was—not home, no. At Mayfield. I wanted to return. To see dear Grandfather, *Grandfather was gone...*

Tessa hovered over me as I tried to sit up. "Oh good, you're finally awake. And if you don't mind my saying it, I could slug Mr. Chinworth, no matter he's a man consequence."

"Why would you do such a thing?" My voice was rusty.

"He drugged you, he did. The cad. Without even asking if you wanted a sip."

I remembered. The news of Grandfather's death, like a knife to my heart. The wine that had been pushed into my hands. "Did I exhibit some grievous fit?"

"No, my lady. You were as regal as any queen upon hearing the sad news." She sniffed. "I've shed my own tears this night. Your grandfather was a good gentleman, despite how he kept you to himself."

"Oh, Tessa. I cannot fathom his death. Do you know more? How it came to be?"

"I've had a letter this morn from his manservant. Wasn't only gout he suffered with."

"I didn't know."

"He kept his struggles to himself until he couldn't. But then, it was too late." Tessa pulled the bell rope. "Do you think you can eat?"

I was surprisingly hungry. "After I dine, we need to set about returning. I must go to my uncles."

Tessa pulled a letter from her pocket. "This also came for you."

"It's in Uncle Richard's hand." I opened the missive, tears building around my eyes.

Dearest Emma,

Our hearts are heavy. You have no doubt received the news of your grandfather's passing. Never have we known a moment without him, how we can move forward will only be by the grace of God. And by His grace, you will live your life without him as well, as hard as the idea may seem.

Do not come home. No, dearest niece. Gerald and I quite agree that it is in your best interest to stay and continue at Mayfield. We feel that doing so honors our brother's desires. We know that honoring his memory by fulfilling his request will also be important to you. We are of one mind and heart on this matter.

There will be no funeral for you to attend, as ladies, especially one such as yourself, would not attend. By the time you read this letter, we shall be walking behind his final carriage dressed in our finest blacks. He will be buried beside your parents. When you are next in London, Lord willing with a husband by your side, you will be welcomed with open arms. We will take you to his gravestone where you may lay your posies.

Give yourself a few days for tears, and then take your handkerchief and tuck it clean-away. Think of yourself. Enjoy your courtship as we know your grandfather will be watching from Heaven and would want you to.

No one gave him greater joy than you, dear one. Nor us.

Ever yours,

Uncle Richard

"They bid me to stay. I don't understand." I truly didn't. "How can I possibly court anyone after such news?"

Tessa pointed to my side table. "The young gentlemen are rather concerned for you. They sent up those flowers—mind you they had to travel all the way to a hothouse in Staffordshire to get them."

Red roses filled a silver cup, another of pink, yet another filled with pale yellow.

"Oh, and Mr. Carter said to give you this." She handed me another envelope from her apron pocket.

I opened a single sheet of paper.

Miss Bartlett,

You've only to say the word and I would be honored to see you home to London. Do not allow any perceived obligations keep you from doing what you feel is best.

J. Carter

I did not know what to do. I felt pulled, like a puppet with strings. Stay and grieve. Stay and do as Grandfather bid. Stay and return – albeit only with a husband at my side. Pressure built in my chest. Grieve, I certainly would. Over more than Grandfather.

I looked to the generous display of roses perfuming the air, then down to Mr. Carter's message. Only one person considered my desires. If only I was certain about them myself.

I spent the day in my room, in a cycle of tears and quiet frustration. I spent a good deal of time gazing from the windows at the sun-shimmered lake. I pondered and prayed. Words were coming more easily now. It had been a fine day. Tessa opened one of the windows and allowed the warm breezes within.

And then we knelt and prayed together for my grieving uncles. How thankful I was for Tessa. As she prayed aloud, I noticed that her words weren't mere memorized words. They sprang straight from her heart. The breeze heightened between us, the scent of spring in the air. God heard me. I knew it as deeply as I knew myself.

I went to my jewelry box and took out the cross of garnets that Grandfather had given me on my seventeenth birthday. I latched it around my neck and tightly held the gems in my hand. I didn't want to forget the truth amid the confusing situation I'd found myself in. I wasn't alone. God was with me.

Later that evening, another glass of wine arrived. I declined to partake. However kind Mr. Chinworth's intentions might have been, the drugged wine had left me disabled with a night full of outlandish dreams. I didn't fancy reliving the horrid experience.

As twilight gave way to night, a chill slipped into the breeze. Clouds gathered and darkened the sky. Veins of lightning struck and shattered the darkness. Gone was my grieving in the peace of a pleasant sun. Thunder shook the ground.

Tessa tossed a shawl around her shoulders and moved to shut the window and curtains. "Who on earth would be out on such a night? They best get inside before they catch their death."

I joined her at the window as lightning brightened the sky for just a second. That was no fisherman. No, indeed. The cut of his dinner jacket gave him away. We saw him again before the sky pummeled rain upon us and blurred our view.

Clearly, one of the Chinworth brothers braved the storm and courted danger. But for what reason? Did he have no fear? Mayhap it was them I saw the first night, not fishermen.

"The man is a lunatic!" Tessa shut the curtains against the flashing light.

I wondered what lay beyond the lake—what made him take such risks? One thing was certain, he wasn't fishing.

Thunder pounced and I blinked to a single, stark fact: I had inherited a fortune. A truth as shocking as the sound of nature. And I wasn't the only one aware of this truth.

No longer in the offing, no longer guarded by the man that was my grandfather. Wholly and entirely, mine. As my uncles were offspring from my great grandfather's second marriage, the inheritance fell at my feet alone.

I sat before the kindled fire and drew close to its flames, warming my chilled hands. I was of an age. I touched the jeweled cross at my neck. *What should I do?*

And with whom?

Chapter Nine

"Miss Bartlett?" Mr. Chinworth craned his neck toward me, then stood. "How good of you to join us for breakfast."

As if I had an option. I had little appetite, but I'd promised Tessa I would eat. "Good morning, and thank you." The breakfast table was empty of the Chinworth brothers. Only Mr. Chinworth and Mr. Carter were there. Refreshing change.

"If my sons had suspected you would be up and about, they would have no doubt appeared." He sat down to his breakfast again while I mindlessly filled my plate.

"I meant to inquire about church and what time service might be." Wondered how he and his boys prioritized religious duties.

"Church?" He swallowed some tea. "I suppose it is Sunday, isn't it? I quite forgot."

Not a good sign.

Mr. Carter pulled my chair and I sat, grateful for his appearance.

"If my sons had any lick of sense..." He left his outward thought unfinished. "Joseph, I suppose you wouldn't mind doing the honors?"

"I'd be happy to escort Miss Bartlett to services, which, I believe begin in two hours." He smiled. "Plenty of time."

I smiled back.

"Good. Braxton will have the carriage sent around."

I wore the darkest dress I owned. A deep blue affair, with an ivory lace fichu—not enough to show myself in mourning. Tessa squeezed my hand. "It is alright. God knows your grief, even if the village cannot see it.

The ancient stone church looked as though it had grown up from the ground with the many surrounding yew trees. I breathed in the brisk air and hoped that I might hear something true of God, a truth to cling to in my pain and shocking change of circumstances.

Not surprisingly, we sat in the Chinworth pew, the man behind the pulpit looked more like a man ready for a boxing ring than to orate upon the word of God. Despite appearances, his firm but gentle voice flowed over me. Had anyone ever spoken with such generous certainty? His work was not a duty but a devotion.

Perhaps I should have stayed tucked within my room another day. Tears aren't meant to be locked away, repressed from spilling but I knew that openly crying during service simply wasn't done. Wasn't seemly.

Mr. Carter must have noticed my distress—his hand found mine beneath my cloak and held fast. His touch strengthened me. How might a true lover's hold feel? Like this, perhaps? Kind, steady, and altogether composed...

After service, Mr. Carter introduced me to the vicar. The man took my gloved hand in his large one and gave it a squeeze. He leaned and murmured in my ear. "He hears you, Miss Bartlett. Never doubt."

My eyes flashed to his. How did he know? How did he decipher the contents of my prayers, the realization of my heart? The answer came.

"Psalm 91, dear heart."

I would look it up when I returned.

He released my hand as Mr. Carter gave me his arm. I felt protected, cared for.

"Joseph?" The vicar's deep, booming voice called out from behind us. "Will we be speaking soon?"

"On the morrow, I hope."

The man nodded. "Well, then, good. I look forward to it."

Nearing Mayfield, Mr. Carter glanced from the window. "What on earth?" Disbelief made him look again.

"What is it?" I looked at Tessa.

"I thought I saw my cousin. Strange. Perhaps I was mistaken." He leaned back in his seat in thought. "Miss Bartlett, I meant what I said in my note."

"Indeed, Mr. Carter. Your words were better to me than hothouse flowers. Far better. I thank you."

He nodded.

Until I knew what I was doing, I had to dance along with pretense about my obligations. A thought bloomed. I might buy a cottage like the one perched on the back of the estate. I so adored it. But just as the thought flowered, it died.

Even if I bought a cottage, it would be a vain purchase without the love of a husband and children to fill it. Despite what society and my uncles thought, I knew that a sense of belonging couldn't be bought. T'was scarce as hen's teeth. In London, I was but a duty – a job – to Mrs. Norris and her daughter, and well I knew it. Like the rest, her affection went only as far as my monetary worth.

Mr. Carter spoke. "Will you take a turn with me in the garden after luncheon? If you don't feel up to it, I quite understand." His eyes pierced me.

Tessa patted my arm. "Fresh air will do you good."

"That sounds lovely. Yes, thank you."

Mr. Carter's smile encouraged. "We might take a turn around the lake if you're interested. Would be best to wear boots. The storm made for a muddy shore."

The air had not quite recovered its spring warmth, but my cloak was quite sufficient against the chill. My courtiers had not come to luncheon either, much to Mr. Chinworth's chagrin. Nonetheless, their absence sent a clear message. His mood had soured and made conversation hard work.

"Would that you were my son, Joseph."

"I am at your disposal, Uncle."

"That you are, lad. That you are." He tossed his napkin aside. "Cecily had a bad night but I think she is awake now. I shall go read to her if you can spare me, my dear?"

"Of course." I nodded.

Donned in cloak and boots, my heart thrummed at the thought of spending more time with Mr. Carter.

No sooner than we were at the edge of the lake than Mr. Carter began in earnest. "You must leave here, Miss Bartlett. I beg you." His voice gained a new urgency there hadn't been before.

How I wanted to comply. "I haven't quite decided. My uncles have insisted I stay."

"What little they know about the true circumstances."

"You never wanted me to come in the first place."

"As you well know."

Yes. And all the reasons he'd explained to me. I chewed my bottom lip, considering what my next steps ought to be. "I won't marry any of them. I promise you."

Relief swam across his eyes.

"But there are other reasons I must abide here."

"What are they?"

I didn't know how to put it into words. "I can't quite make sense of it. I've been praying...Grandfather's death was so unexpected, I—"

"Forgive me." He paused our walk and looked down at me. "You need time. None of us expected you to come out of your rooms so early. Grief must work its course. But I believe your grandfather's death makes it all the more urgent that you leave."

"Am I not in control of my own destiny now?" What was his meaning?

"Miss Bartlett, I'm trying to help you stay in control of that destiny. My cousins will pursue you until one of them gains you." The lines of his lips drew a straight line.

Never did I think courtship and marriage to be such a threat. "You make it sound as though I have a target on my back."

He grinned wryly. "And when they have gained your hand in marriage, you will no longer be in control of your future."

The fact pressed. Cold and strange. My husband would be in charge of the whole of it. No more choices, only directives. The inheritance, my life. My doings, comings, and goings...wouldn't be mine to decide. Would my future mate be as withdrawn as Grandfather? Would I be fastened in one place, never to leave?

"If there's one thing you need, it's some freedom for a change."

He understood. And he was right. Emotion lodged in my throat. I missed my grandfather, yet I yearned for experience. I wanted to pick wildflowers. Race down a grassy slope like a child. Sing at the top of my lungs. "There is much I'd like to do." My mind whirled.

"Where would you like to start?"

My eyes burned. "I have long desired to step into the ocean."

"Step into the ocean, huh?" He smiled.

"I want to feel the sand between my bare toes."

"Scandalous, Miss Bartlett." His eyes shone.

"Oh. Is it?" Had I been harboring a licentious desire?

"No," he laughed, "I jest with you."

I stumbled and he tightened his hold. "Tell me, what else would you do?"

"Spend entire days out of doors with a picnic and a sketch-book. Go berry picking." A tear fell, and then another.

"And?"

"I'd ride horses every day, and ride like the wind. I'd climb a tree if it wasn't too dangerous." My vision now blurred beyond sight. "I'd make friends and I'd embrace them as they would embrace me. We'd sit before a large fire together and toast bread, and laugh, and..." I'd been too open. I'd let him see my heart. The things I'd longed for but had always been forced to repress. I couldn't stop the flow of tears, hot and full of heartache.

His arm alighted softly around my shoulders, he pressed his handkerchief into my hand. "What you desire sounds heavenly."

I swiped at the unrelenting flow. "Grandfather wouldn't allow for such frivolity. For any of it." I was a lady of London. An heiress. Resigned to a genteel life that didn't have room for these frivolous wants.

Mr. Carter took a deep breath. "Something kept him from living life as it's meant to be lived. I think he was afraid for you, after the accident."

"Yes. That must be true." That and more. He cared too much about his money. Didn't want me to waste a farthing.

"He hid his greatest treasure away for safekeeping." We paused within a gap in a willow tree with sweeping fronds dusting the ground in the breeze. His warm eyes, reassuring. "He loved you more than anything else. How could he not?"

We faced the lake as clouds slid away from the afternoon sun, allowing its brightness to soak into me until I was warm.

I, the greatest treasure? Fear, then, was a terrible trap. Whoever meant to cause us harm, did so with far-reaching consequences.

"Remain here at Mayfield as long as you need, Miss Bartlett. But do let me know if the conquests become too difficult." His jaw clenched tightly. "If they were honorable men, I wouldn't bat an eye—"

I finished for him. "If they pursued me because of my inheritance. I wouldn't feel any better."

"Honor makes everything better. If they were truly honorable, pursuing you would be about more than that."

"But not less than."

"No. You have a point. You are quite right."

We reached a copse of trees.

"Last I looked, there was a berry bramble just on the other side—" his words halted. There, propped against a wide tree trunk in the thick of low grass, was Samuel.

"Oh my. Is he asleep?" Why did he look so strange?

Head tossed back, his eyes were closed. Saliva dripped from his chin, a brown jug cradled in his hands. His jacket was missing, his cravat lay curved about the brambles like a snake, and his vest and shirt lay open, exposing his bare chest.

"Behold, your knight in shining armor." Mr. Carter gestured before turning around. "I think it best to let him come to his senses on his own, don't you think?" He led me away.

"What is wrong with him?"

"Have you never seen a drunk man before?"

I hadn't. "I've heard a few men singing rather ridiculous-ly—in the middle of the night as they passed down our street."

"Samuel is well past singing."

He released me at the entry of the house. "I must inform his manservant to send a wheelbarrow around to gather him up."

I giggled at the picture.

"He won't feel so humorous when he wakes."

"Thank you for the walk, Mr. Carter. You are kindness itself." I curtsied.

He bowed but stood and gazed at me as if wanting to say more. His eyes held me in place. I hoped upon hope that I could trust him. I broke away and climbed the long stairway to my room alone.

That evening, Tessa answered a knock at my door. She curtsied and turned to me. "We have been invited downstairs to the small parlor."

I'd already donned my nightgown and robe. I dreaded seeing the Chinworths, knowing the game they'd play to gain me. But I couldn't be rude to my host. "Very well." I shed my sleep garb and put on an old, plain day gown instead of an evening dress.

I followed Tessa to the room indicated. It was a smaller room, little used, jutting off from the grand library. We entered and found Mr. Carter standing by a low fire of bright coals, toasting fork in hand. His coat had been tossed to a chair, his shirt sleeves rolled up as though he had work to do.

A sliced loaf of bread sat near a large square of butter. Delicious possibilities awaited.

"And this, Miss Bartlett, is when you begin to live as you desire." He handed me the long fork. "If you're willing to count me as a friend, that is."

I accepted the fork, and yes, indeed, his friendship. I glanced at Tessa.

"Shall I toast the bread for you, my lady?"

"You may toast your own and also be my friend?" Was it possible? What would I have done without her?

"You shall always have my friendship, my lady."

We knelt upon the rug, each of us holding our forks to the flames. Mr. Carter on one side, Tessa on my other. Like companions I'd read about in stories. True friends.

Unlike the aristocratic Norris's whose backs would never touch chairs, never a hair out of place, nor a manner at odds with custom. Kneeling on the rug before the fire felt more real than anything I'd ever done.

A few contented hours later, I walked into my private parlor to have a word with Tessa. She bent before the snapping hearth and tossed a folded bit of paper within. She stepped inside her room and shut the door. She hadn't noticed me.

I quickly walked to where she'd been and knelt to see. There, flaming in the hot coals were the words: *Emmaline must marry as soon as possible. In all haste...see to it...*

What? Was I betrayed?

Uncle Richard's hand was unmistakable.

Why the haste? And why should Tessa be involved? I didn't understand. Not one bit. The pleasurable hours I'd just enjoyed soured. Tessa hid something from me, else why burn the message?

The words of my uncle resounded in my mind as I left Chatswick. *"Thank goodness, she's gone."* Tessa had rushed me away from the door. Had she heard it too?

I left the parlor, crawled into bed, and pulled the blankets tightly around me. A few things were certain. My uncles wanted me to marry quickly. Equally certain: I wouldn't marry a Chinworth.

Why were they glad that I'd gone?

Why did they want me to marry as soon as possible?

Had they enlisted Tessa to reach their goal?

And why had Mr. Carter reentered my life? Was he truly to be trusted?

A weightier question lingered... *Who had chased my parents to their deaths...?*

Chapter Ten

I should have thought better of a lonely garden stroll. But I'd needed fresh air after spending the better part of the day being tossed back and forth like a cricket ball between Zachary and Tobias.

I stood stock still as three of the four wolf hounds bounded over to me. I took a deep breath and looked behind my shoulder. I had no rescuer.

I trembled as I held out my hand, stiff and straight. "Sit."

They did! Immediately, the trio sat at my command, rising as high as my waist. I took a breath of relief. They wouldn't attack. What was I supposed to do now in this sea of dogs? I dare not turn my back to them and I wasn't ready to offer a friendly pat let alone rigorous play.

"You might have the world at your feet if you entered society like a normal woman of means." Samuel. Rocks crunched beneath his boots as he made his way towards me. Where had he come from? Behind that hedge?

"A normal woman of means?" He insinuated that I was abnormal. So be it.

"Just saying." He lifted a rare smile. "If I'd seen you in London, I would have asked you to dance. More than once."

His inference wasn't lost on me. To dance more than once with a gentleman signified more...I offered a smile of my own. "If Grandfather had allowed the introduction."

"Ah, but he has, hasn't he?"

I'd lost my train of thought. He blocked the sun, his steel blue eyes and confident gaze demanded my attention. He wanted me to acknowledge, out in the open, my grandfather's plans to marry one of them, nay, to choose and marry.

"So instead of the usual dance, we must play at a complicated minuet where my brothers and I woo you, and you do the asking." He drew closer, his scent of bergamot filled the gap between us. He took a deep breath and lowered his voice. "You are aware that I am the oldest?"

He would inherit, in his own right. The vast estate spread before us.

"We could join forces and live like royalty." He pulled a deep red rose from his inner pocket and handed it to me. I pretended not to notice that it was crushed. "How shall you bear it, I wonder?" He winked. "Think on it, Miss Bartlett, what we might become, together..."

One of the wolf hounds snuffled my hand and placed his furry head beneath it, a steadier presence than the man before me.

He looked down at the beast. "Seems we all quite like you. Man and animal."

"Mr. Chinworth, you are too generous." Both in thought and expectation. "How are you feeling today?"

"Pardon?"

"After finding you unconscious in the woods, I was quite undone as to your condition."

"My condition?" He looked startled. "Wait, of what do you speak?"

"Brown jugs and missing cravats, Mr. Chinworth. Unwieldly things, I imagine. Gets in the way of better intentions, however small." I curtsied and turned away. "Good afternoon."

I turned from him, his mouth agape. He quickly caught up to me at the water fountain. "Miss Bartlett." He pressed a hand to his heart. "It does you credit to care. I most sincerely thank you. I was indeed unwell. How terrible for you to find me thus. The storm sent my head into an ache that I could not cure."

Had he been the one by the lake? That night? No wonder his head hurt.

He boldly took my hand and kissed the back of it. "I assure you that I am much recovered."

I remained mum.

He bowed again and made his way to the stables. A very handsome man, indeed. But his offerings fell flat. By joining our inheritances, we'd have more. More of what I already had? To me, it amounted to nothing.

I plucked the red rose apart, petal by petal until only pieces lay at my feet. Red roses belonged to true lovers. Not Samuel and I. Not ever.

An hour later, I'd been swept into a hack where Tobias sped along the country roads. Tessa jostled on the seat behind us. He stopped the horse and led me up a green hill that bore a significantly large oak tree. Spring leaves unfurled a tender green. The sky, a bright blue.

Tobias winked as his brother had done and whispered. "If only we could get rid of *her*..." He glanced at Tessa who huffed her way alone up the steep path. No gentleman he.

"I'm glad that we shall not."

His brows rose. "You are? Say it isn't true."

He imagined that I wanted to be alone with him. I tried to draw his attention away from me. "This tree is magnificent." The view from the top, absolutely stunning.

He ignored my comment and stumbled on. "I know I'm not the oldest—"

"Birth order doesn't signify the quality of a person." Nor does his or her inheritance. Or how handsome the gentleman happened to be.

His eyes shuttered halfway, his voice lowered, "You are quite right."

I hadn't meant to encourage him. Needed to learn to bite my tongue.

He smiled and cast his gaze on the expanse of the countryside before us. "Father has given me a small estate, twenty miles north of here."

Was he bragging? "So far?"

"Sadly."

"Are you often there? Do you oversee its management?"

"Not at all." He swatted a fly. "My steward handles it for me. The tenants make a menace of themselves. Always wanting this or that. Never satisfied. They can never have enough."

"How inconvenient for you."

"Quite."

His lack of character rose to the surface with such ease. Mr. Carter had thought I could be easily swayed by these gentlemen. On the contrary. Poor Grandfather was self-deceived to think that any Chinworth heir would be worth his salt.

Tobias tapped the end of a horsewhip in his gloved hand. "Did your grandfather own estates?"

Did he? I gazed across the distant fields of sheep, trying to spot the shepherdess of my fantasy. His question gave me pause. Other than Chatswick, I knew of none. But that was entirely expected. Titled men owned estates. More than one.

Tessa gained my side with a handful of violets. "Lord Bartlett owned but one besides Chatswick. And a lodge in Wales, I believe."

News to me. Surprise fluttered across my middle. Two properties to my name? I could scarcely believe it. Grandfather—and my uncles never spoke of them. At least not within my hearing.

I needed to speak with my grandfather's solicitor. Did I have control over these estates even now? Were the tenants in Wales properly cared for? Perhaps Mr. Carter would know.

If only I'd known that Chinworth had invited company to dinner, I might have been able to ease my mind about it. How had no one seen fit to inform me of our guests sooner?

I played my part as best as I could. The middle-aged neighbors would have been a bright spot in the week had my anxiety over the details of Grandfather's estate not formed a tightening knot in my mind. Though they were kind and attentive, especially by comparison to the Chinworth boys, I fidgeted the evening through. Finding the opportunity to talk to Mr. Carter proved difficult.

He was late to dinner, then his time was monopolized by the gentleman who desired to brag about his latest acquisition of a set of pistols used in a famous duel, between none other than the famous Lord Banbury and some long-deceased Baron from Ulster.

I cringed at the name. After Grandfather's story, I perused the newspapers. He'd been called the King of Scandal. A tyrant.

Blessedly, the couple finally left. I tried to find a way to speak with Mr. Carter, but he'd disappeared altogether. I tried another avenue. Mr. Chinworth, longtime friend of Grandfather, would be certain to assist me.

"Mr. Chinworth, I know it is late, but might I have a word?"

"Indeed, Miss Bartlett." He motioned to the settee. "Let us sit."

His sons had made quick bows to me a moment before. And then they gave me their backs. The card table held a greater enticement for them—and I sighed at the welcome relief from their company.

I sat, uncertain how to proceed. I knew little of what I needed to ask. "As you are aware, I have inherited a great deal."

He didn't flinch at my openness. "Indeed, my dear." His eyes seemed to brighten.

"Since much now rests upon my shoulders, I think I should speak with Grandfather's solicitor. I feel it is of utmost importance."

"Why certainly, you do, Miss Bartlett." He rubbed his hands and pressed his lips together. "Your grandfather, good soul, never intended that you should carry the weight alone."

"I believe you are right." I couldn't bring myself to tell him that I'd never be engaged to any of his sons. In retrospect, I should have made that fact plain.

"I must go to London. Will you arrange a carriage—say in two days?" He didn't quite answer me.

"Ah, my dear. Must you travel?" He shook his head. "Will not a letter suffice?"

"There are too many details I need to understand." He didn't know how truly ignorant I was of Grandfather's business. Tenants might depend upon my holdings. "I must insist."

"Of course. I will do all that I can to help you." The line of his lips grew straight and serious. I believed him, this good friend of Grandfather's. "Not to worry, my dear. Not to worry."

He patted my hand and bade me goodnight.

The next morning I was to leave, I took a long swallow of tea at the breakfast table. I know not what happened next.

In barely a blink, I became heavy. So heavy. My limbs were weighed down, my eyelids refused to lift until a familiar voice bid them to obey.

"Open up."

Tessa? My friend?

"Raise her head. That's it." Liquid poured between my teeth. Warm and sweet. I gulped the drink and darkness swallowed me.

I woke with a start in the middle of the night. So confused. Where was I? Had I not been on my way to London? What prevented me from leaving?

The last thing I remembered was getting dressed for travel—I'd been preparing to see Grandfather's solicitor. I'd gone down to breakfast, but only drank tea—and then—nothing.

Mr. Chinworth.

He'd drugged me again. How dare I allow myself to be fooled twice?

But why? Did he intend for me to marry one of his petulant sons? I remembered Tessa's voice, her urging me to drink. She had helped them. That was clear.

Lord, I prayed, as I looked out from those windows at the starry night. *What can I do?*

Mr. Carter had urged me to leave and I'd chosen to stay. Why? I should have listened. Out of curiosity, I tried my bedroom door handle. Locked.

Fear plunged its knife into my middle. I was trapped. One way or another, the Chinworths were determined to have my inheritance—and my freedom. And who would know? Who would miss me?

I moved to my parlor door and tried the handle. Open. One more door to try—the one that led to the hallway. I touched the cold metal and twisted. A gear clicked, but the latch gave way.

This door had been locked too, but not latched properly. I left it slightly ajar. Thank God.

If I had any qualms about running from this place before, they were gone now. My trunk had been unpacked and my things put away. As though I'd never meant to leave. How long had I been asleep? A day? A week?

Dressing quietly, and with cumbersome movements, I gathered a few necessities within a small reticule. I stepped quietly into the hall.

I prayed no servants were awake. Nor a drunken Samuel to bar me from leaving. I walked down the hall, along the edges where the floors would be firm and make less noise. A trick I'd learned at home. The stairs were easily managed. With a pounding heart, I headed for the side door that led to the garden. My path to freedom.

The opening was my key to escape. I breathed in the cool night air. For better or worse, I was on my own. The Chinworths meant me ill. Tessa betrayed her faithful service to me. And where had Mr. Carter gone? Did he not notice my absence and demand to see me? How I hoped that to be the case.

I swallowed down tears. Now was not the time for pity. It would only slow me down. I stepped onto the path leading to the road. And from there? God would be my guide.

Hands wrapped around my middle and pulled me back. Another hand pressed tightly against my mouth to prevent me from screaming. Fear weakened my limbs, blackness filled my vision. The man whispered. "Sh... we *must* be quiet. It's me, Miss Bartlett. We must stay behind this tree. Don't move. Please."

Mr. Carter? My heart slowed to a firm knocking. Would he trap me here like the others? No. I wrestled against him.

"I beg you, calm yourself. I mean you no harm."

Was he telling the truth? I knew fighting against him, either way, would do no good.

His hold gentled. "Can I trust you not to scream?"

I nodded.

"Good. We must bend low. Come." I sank with him by the tree roots, his arm stayed wrapped around me, firm and steadying. I leaned closer.

A horse galloped nearer, entering the carriage track from the field, another followed. A set of footsteps sounded from the path I'd just walked. How close I'd been to being caught.

"Well?"

Samuel's voice was unmistakable. "She will be dead soon. And then I will be free to marry Miss Bartlett."

Another cursed. Zachary. "If not? If she recovers?"

"One can hope."

"What of the child?" Zachary spoke as though through gritted teeth.

"No one knows about it."

"You are heartless." Tobias was angry. "The boy is yours, Samuel. You cannot pretend otherwise."

"You worry too much. Miss Bartlett would be a fool not to choose me, and you well know it."

I tightened as my name was repeated.

"She's turned your head and made you dumb. Mark my words, she won't be having you, Tobs."

"You are *already married*." Tobias again.

"What? You in love with her already?"

"He's in love with her fortune, as we all are. It's quite beautiful to contemplate."

"Father should have told us sooner." Samuel snickered. "May the best man win. And be assured that I certainly plan to."

They hushed as a stable hand approached and led the horses away.

Zachary cleared his throat. "What if she'll have none of us?"

"Father has made certain that she won't leave until she chooses." Samuel again.

I trembled. The web was pulling tighter.

Urgency laced Tobias's voice. "If the girl ever wakes up, that is. Would be a tragedy if he gave her too much and—"

I was right. I hadn't been merely ill or out of my mind. I'd been drugged exactly as when Grandfather died.

Samuel laughed. "You've given me the best idea."

"You wouldn't."

"Wouldn't I? Put her out of her misery? The poor lass suffers. Would be a mercy."

"You'd murder your own wife?"

"Eh? Chances are, I won't have to, she's that ill."

"Let's get to bed. We have a long week of wooing ahead. Father insists that one of us captures her hand by the week's end."

"Five days left," Zachary grumbled.

A yawn, a boot shifted in the gravel. A swear. They left what they thought was a private discussion and stepped as quietly into the house as I had left it.

"Dear God." Mr. Carter whispered. "Are you alright?"

I nodded, too stunned for words. The plan was finally revealed.

"Now you see why I insisted you leave?"

"Horrible..." Words choked in my throat.

"Yes." He assessed me, shivering from shock or cold, I didn't know which. He put his coat around my shoulders. His warmth enveloped me, his scent of evergreen calmed.

What would happen next? If only I'd known not to trust Mr. Chinworth. "Where have you been the last few days?"

Mr. Carter brushed a hair from my face, loosened from my struggling. "I might ask you the same. Tessa said you were ill, taken to your bed."

"I tried to leave, as you recommended. I asked Mr. Chinworth for a carriage to take me to London. To talk to Grandfather's solicitor. He agreed. Said he'd do anything to help me."

"What?" He pulled me to my feet. "Come, let's find a place where there won't be a chance of being overheard."

He led me across the dark front lawn then right—into the woods and the stone folly. The Grecian woman, frozen in the moonlight. Seeing nothing, going nowhere. We sat on the cold benches. The one man I could trust nearby.

He kept my hands within his, cold from the night air. I'd forgotten my gloves. He rubbed them slowly between his palms. "I wish you'd come to me first."

"I tried, but you were late to dinner that night—then gone before I could talk to you."

"Mm." His hands stilled. "I was at Goodwyn Abbey with my student. Why the urgency to meet with your Grandfather's solicitor? I've no doubt he has everything in hand for you."

"Do you know about my other property?"

"Property?" Mr. Carter was honestly confused.

"Tessa seemed to know, yet I've never heard a single word about a lodge in Wales, apart from Chatswick. I was concerned about possible tenants on my lands—are they cared for? Indeed. Zachary seemed to disdain his. I could never ignore the poor souls."

"I can safely say that your lands are empty of tenants, save a skeleton staff to care for the estate."

"That is a relief. There's so much I don't know—and don't understand. I had no indication that Mr. Chinworth would go to such lengths to deny my request."

"You became ill? Fainted?"

"No. Drugged. By them."

Fury flashed across his face. "So that's what he meant by my uncle making sure you wouldn't leave." His jaw tightened. "Unthinkable. How dare he? Tell me how it happened."

"I was about to take my leave. Tessa had packed my trunk and all was ready to go. I wanted to tell you, but you'd gone. I didn't know where I might send a message." I shuddered at the memory. "I went down to breakfast—and the last thing I remember was taking tea."

"I cannot believe it—but for the word of his son, who has now implicated him."

He wouldn't let me leave until I'd chosen one. And married him.

"They must be desperate to take such measures."

"And Tessa," I continued. "I know I cannot trust her."

His hold on my hands grew stiff.

"Are you certain? What has she done?"

"She gave me more of the drug. I was half-lucid, but I recall her begging me to swallow. Darkness claimed me yet again."

"Perhaps she didn't know you'd been drugged in the first place. Nor does she control what is placed in your tea."

"I might believe you except I saw her burn a letter from my uncle. She didn't know I'd seen her do it. When I looked into the ashes, I saw a few words that gave me caution." My throat had gone dry, my voice raspy. "She is to influence my marriage—in all haste."

Mr. Carter released my hands and pulled a flask from his coat. "Here, drink."

I hesitated.

"It is only water."

I wavered. What if I became unconscious again? I pegged this moment in my memory so that I wouldn't forget. At least I'd know who to trust. I tipped my head back and drank. It was indeed water. I felt nothing untoward.

I handed the flask back to him.

"Go ahead, drink the rest." Though my thirst was quenched, I felt a weakness in my limbs, but not from the water. The drugs had exhausted my strength. The shock of the night, my attempt at escaping...

"I wouldn't condemn Tessa quite yet, Miss Bartlett."

Why ever not? "Did I mention that I'd been locked in my rooms?"

"What?" He put his arm around me again. "You tremble so."

"When I awoke, I suspected what had happened. Knew I had to leave immediately. When I tried my door handles..." I shook my head. "Thankfully, the sitting room door hadn't been latched properly."

"And that's when you made your way outside and I found you."

"Narrowly escaping the Chinworth brothers." Such a tangled scandal.

Mr. Carter placed his hand beneath my chin. "I must ask you now to be brave. Can you bear to stay a few days longer?"

What choice did I have?

Chapter Eleven

"But why will you not help me? I thought you wanted me to leave. I must escape." Panic rose, despite the welcome warmth of his touch. If only I'd paid attention to my unease back in London, when he warned me, pled with me not to come. Had I listened I wouldn't be in this situation. I would have been by Grandfather's side before he died. Except apparently —my uncles, my dear, dear uncles didn't want me there. "I must speak with my solicitor. I cannot trust this household. Or my own maid."

He reached out. "You can trust Tessa." He released my chin.

"But she—"

"Has no intention to influence you to marry a Chinworth. Which is why she burned that letter."

"How do you know?" What if she really did know my tea had been drugged?

"Because I recruited her."

Recruited her? "Grandfather hired her after my governess left. She'd been with me for two years."

"I made sure she had credentials that your Grandfather couldn't refuse."

"I still don't understand."

His brow furrowed. "Someone had to look out for you, Miss Bartlett."

"A spy for—you?"

"Not a spy. A protector. And a true friend."

"She reported to you about the little heiress you'd saved?" How bitter my voice sounded. I didn't like not knowing these details. Too many secrets kept.

My sharp words didn't affect him. "Only to inform me of your happiness and welfare. Nothing more."

"I see." But I didn't, and he knew. He could tell how I felt.

Tears flowed. My situation was in a tangle when all I wanted was to know my place in this world. And put my toes in the sand of an ocean... That wasn't too much to ask.

"I don't begrudge you your grief, Emma. I'm truly sorry."

"Why won't you help me leave now? Didn't you tell me that I only need say the word?"

"I did." He sighed. "A day ago, it would have been possible. But if we leave now, Emma, they will only follow us."

"And?"

"I must ask you to trust me once again. What we heard moments ago is so troubling, I cannot let it go unchallenged."

"Samuel is married." I pulled my handkerchief from my sleeve and dabbed my eyes.

"As I suspected for some time now." He faced me again, "I fear he plans great evil."

I chilled within his hold.

Murder. And more.

"The sun will begin to rise in a few hours. We must make our own plans."

Before I slipped back into my sitting room, back into my nightgown, back into bed—I knew what I needed to do.

"Pretend you've woken, with no memory of your great expectation to leave. Allow my cousins to court you. Be the beautiful heiress come to choose her mate. I will inform Tessa to be vigilant."

Could I really play this part? "Why can you not send a constable to arrest Samuel?"

"I can't very well accuse a man of a crime yet to be committed. If you try to leave now, Samuel, in desperation, may do the deed before I can stop him."

"What will you do?"

"Find the wife and child and get them to safety."

"What if something happens while you're gone?"

"I will teach you to defend yourself."

"With a pistol?"

"Heavens, no." That smile of his quirked at his lips. I'd grown fond of that grin. "Not yet, at least."

Time grew short and I had to wait. Mr. Carter made sure I arrived to my bedroom without incident. I put the contents of my bundle back in place and crawled into bed. I thirsted but shirked the half-empty tea cup that sat within reach.

I tried to close my eyes and sleep, but the night's events replayed. Samuel's treachery... I thought of the poor woman whom he'd made a wife and hoped would die soon. Of his innocent child. Without a mother.

The minister said that God heard my prayers. It was true. I believed that. I couldn't close my eyes to sleep but would close them to pray.

I lay there and wept. For the young woman who suffered. I prayed God to keep her safe. I prayed that Mr. Carter found her quickly—and that she would be healed of her illness. I prayed that God would keep Samuel's hands from evil and bring him to his knees. Repentant, heart open.

And then, I prayed for Cecily. I'd paid her little to no attention while here, so self-absorbed I'd been. The neglected sister who'd been put out of sight and mind... No wonder she'd turned out as she had. Poor thing. The child had to be as lonely as I'd been. I'd find a new purpose for my days besides pretending to court.

I blinked my eyes open from my prayer as Tessa came to my side. "Thank God, you're awake."

I stretched my arms wide, with a real yawn. "I feel as though I slept for days." Trust her, Mr. Carter's voice replayed in my mind. I would comply.

Tessa lay a hand on my shoulder. "You were that unwell." She pulled the bell. "I imagine you are starving."

She walked to the door and twisted the lock. The lock that latched from within. I'd been a fool. In my panic, I'd assumed the worst of her. How foolish of me.

"I felt it best to stay bolted in last night." She began to go through my frocks hanging in the wardrobe. "I wasn't sure, but

I thought Mr. Chinworth may have had the housekeeper doctor your drink again."

I drew up to sit against the headboard. "Oh?"

"He said you'd gone ill at breakfast and quite fainted."

"Indeed, I do not remember." That was true.

"From here on out, I will prepare your tea. Only I." She smiled. "If you really are ill, I will do the instructing. You may be sure, I've already had a talk with the housekeeper." She pulled a cream and peach gown from the hanger. "Now, do you feel quite yourself today? No queasy stomach, no headache?"

"None whatsoever."

"I wouldn't have you medicated if you no longer had need of it."

A message arrived along with breakfast. For Tessa? She slid the seal and unfolded the paper.

"I see. Well, I am glad of it." She handed me the message—from Mr. Carter. Only two words filled the blank space: *She knows.*

"When you get back on your feet." She slipped the note from my fingers and tossed it into the fire. "We'll see about leaving for London as you planned."

"In time." I accepted the breakfast tray, sans tea, and ate. Surely nothing nefarious had been hidden within my scone. "I think it would be best to stay a little longer." I hoped justice to be swift.

Tessa wiped the inside of our teacups with a clean cloth, then prepared the tea. She sipped her cup first. And waited. "Perfectly good." She filled the other cup and handed it to me. "Go ahead."

The steaming hot amber fluid strengthened me. There was a life to save, and as Mr. Carter said, I had my part to play in her rescue. Whatever crazy story I found myself in the midst of, I'd discovered, wasn't solely my own. My actions or inactions could affect another. Wasn't her life as valuable as mine?

The thought humbled me. I would do as Mr. Carter desired. "I believe I shall join the family today, Tessa. But do stay close by."

"Yes, my lady."

"Please, when we are alone, call me by my name."

"Very well." She smiled.

The family was surprised to see me at luncheon. Tessa had taken extra time with my hair. My gown, she said complimented my skin so well that I looked like a sun-kissed peach. I appeared ready to play the courting game.

My new purpose had quite taken hold of me. My confidence grew with each step I took. The gentlemen stood, including Mr. Carter.

"How well you look, my dear!" said Mr. Chinworth. "Why, none would guess you've been ill upon your bed for two days, at least!"

"I am quite recovered, I assure you." I curtsied. "Must have been something I ate." Or drank, more like.

"Sit, sit." He pulled the empty chair beside him. "Samuel will fill your plate for you, dear."

One of the maids filled my cup with tea, then refilled Mr. Carter's cup and Tobias's cup from the same pot. I looked at Mr. Carter who shook his head ever so slightly. Some noxious substance must have already been placed within mine before she poured. I would forgo it, thankful for his warning.

Samuel set my plate before me with a murmur in my ear. "Walk with me after?"

I nodded. "Very well." The more time he spent with me, the less he was able to hurt his wife. Or harm his innocent child. While I was resolved, I was afraid. My confidence wavered. The little poem about the spider and the fly rose to surface. Who was which? Time would tell.

"I should like to take tea with Cecily today if she is up for it." I caught Zachary's eye-roll. But Mr. Chinworth appeared delighted by the idea.

"Oh, she certainly will be overjoyed to have your company, I am sure." He offered me what seemed to be a genuine smile. "How good of you to consider her."

It shouldn't be good of anyone to consider another lonely soul, but rather a normal habit. One I supposed I needed to develop, as my life has ever been at my own disposal—between the walls of Chatswick, that is. No commendations were necessary. As lonely as I'd been, I found myself to be at fault for what I had lacked. Had I pursued Tessa's friendship sooner? I would have known less loneliness, more trust.

My tea-taking with Cecily was not to be the philanthropic event I imagined. Oh no, opening the door to her nursery quite turned out to be a Pandora's box of unforeseen consequences. The sickly-sweet pink walls of her bedroom pressed in on all sides. The gold-gilt furniture was that of a demanding little queen who had anything she'd ever wanted.

Cecily's blue eyes, round and innocent, bargained like the devil. I was stuck in my chair with no remedy, or excuse to offer. She sat across from me with a smug, tight smile.

"I saw you in the folly last night."

My stomach plunged a sickening drop. "Perhaps you were dreaming."

Her brows furrowed together. "Do not patronize me." Her tea sat untouched. "I am often at the folly, especially at night." She leaned forward. "I sneak away from Nurse and pretend that I can do whatever I wish. At least for a short time..."

"Are you sure you saw me there?"

"I'm not blind." She cocked her head, her long, blonde hair falling across one shoulder. "Or deaf."

I wasn't sure what to say. How long had she been there and how much had she heard?

"Oh, I haven't told anyone. Don't worry." She fingered a low arrangement of roses in the center of the table. A steep expense for one so young. "Samuel gave me these. Samuel gives me many things."

"I imagine your brother loves you very much."

She shrugged her shoulders. "Zachary and Tobias don't."

"I'm sure you are mistaken." Yes, we must speak on other things. And quickly.

"I'm not." She sipped her tea, sloshing some in her cup when the door opened. Her nurse brought in a tray of ginger cake and lemon sauce, setting it down between us. She curtsied and left.

Cecily paled a little. At being overheard by her nurse? Possibly. She leaned forward. "Your reputation will be in tatters if I tell." Her brows lifted. "And you'll be forced to marry my poor cousin since you've been caught alone with him at night. Propriety matters in such situations. You'll have lost your chance with Samuel." She sipped her tea again, driving home her point. Samuel inherited. And she, like everyone else, thought, incorrectly, that I cared about their riches. How unlikely, when I didn't even care about my own.

Forced to marry her cousin? I wasn't sure I'd mind one whit. My face burned at her suggestion. Our secret talks had been necessary, and Mr. Carter had been nothing but a gentleman.

She refilled my cup as stiffly as Mrs. Norris in London when determined to win at whist. "You *will* choose Samuel," she set the pot down, "or I will ruin you with the truth. Father will be furious at your foolish choices."

The lass didn't know that someone as wealthy as I could hardly be ruined. Disinvited to social events? I'd never been welcomed as it was. No, I am most worried about Samuel's wife. Cecily must not have heard that. How her beloved brother thought to murder her to free himself to marry me.

The longer I sat in her presence, I realized that she hadn't heard any of my conversation with Mr. Carter. She'd merely spied us alone within the folly. And that was enough to bargain for what she wanted, which seemed like Samuel's happiness.

An odd thing for a child to desire. Samuel was a grown man who had plenty of things to do besides spend his time placating her. Buying her loyalty. Had she a deep affection for him because he gave her the most attention? Must be.

The question niggled. "What is it you really want, dear?"

Her face turned red, "I'm not your *dear*." The biting words returned. "You have fouled your reputation. I'm giving you a chance to redeem yourself."

Redemption had nothing to do with the silver of betrayal.

"May I be assured of your cooperation? You will allow Samuel to court you?"

I nodded, what else could I do? If she told of my midnight tryst? I couldn't bear to think of the consequences. Samuel's secret wife, his child—even my own life hung in the balance.

"Good. See that you do. You have until sundown Saturday to accept an engagement from him. And only him." She placed a hand upon her forehead and her fingers trembled. "Or you'll be stuck with poor, poor Joseph. Yuck." She pushed her bottom lip out, imagining my dismay. "I've a headache." She rang the bell and her nurse arrived with another tray.

She handed Cecily a small glass of water, which she downed obediently. A moment later, the trembling subsided and the child slumped asleep upon folded arms. The nurse carried her into the next room and lay her on her bed.

"What have you given her?" Clearly, it worked quickly.

"An elixir to keep her from seizing, Miss." She tucked blankets around her. "Keeps her right calm. It's for her own good."

I'd noticed the same result when Grandfather had taken his medicine. And when I had been unwittingly given mine...the elixir worked quickly. Too quickly.

Last night, Zachary had intimated that it would be a pity if I didn't wake. That too much of that potion would see me dead. It had given Samuel the idea to end his wife's life more swiftly—and easily. She'd fall asleep and no one would be the wiser.

No—surely not. But the thought had formed and I couldn't shake the possibility. Had someone given Grandfather the same and ended his life? So that I would inherit all the sooner?

I withdrew from the room. So many questions. I needed to find Mr. Carter.

CHAPTER TWELVE

I rounded the corner of the stables, looking for him. And only him. A pair of grasping hands steadied me when I tripped on a flagstone. Zachary's. He smiled widely.

"Just the person I most hoped to see." He stood too close, the stink of alcohol on his breath.

Mr. Chinworth had given his sons until the end of the week to make a claim on me. Cecily had done the same, insisting on Samuel. Or else. I reminded myself that only I had the final decision.

I sought refuge near the stable hands. I would not be alone with any of these men again if I could help it. My walk with Samuel earlier had been rife with smooth compliments and transparent attempts to get me to promise to dance with him at an upcoming ball.

I didn't remind him I couldn't dance as I was in mourning. Shouldn't have to. Tessa had sent for black dresses, but they hadn't arrived. Would I be forced to attend? Likely.

The stable hand mounted the horse and rode away. We were alone again. Unwanted solitude indeed. I wondered at Cecily's choice of brothers. With no siblings to dote upon, this was a family state I'd often envied. But not today.

Zachary wrapped his hand around my wrist and drew me near, his dark eyes searching mine. "Don't you like me?" He wobbled like a hobby horse, his breath reeked. "Am I not more handsome than my Shamuel?" His brows lifted as he tried to focus.

I tried to pull away but could not. "Please, let me go!"

"You like me, I know it." He pulled me closer, his other arm wrapped around my waist, his unshaven jaw uncomfortably close. I pushed back with all my might.

A voice shouted, another joined it. Mr. Carter yelled and ran towards me, Samuel on his heels.

"Please help me." I pulled once again as pain shot up my arm.

"You're scaring her, you buffoon!" Samuel jerked Zachary's grip from my wrist, his fingernails leaving two angry red trails.

Mr. Carter pushed Zachary who lost balance, stumbling to his backside.

Mr. Carter flicked his chin in disgust. "Not the way to treat a lady."

Samuel stood, arms folded, over his sneering brother. "Come, why are you in your cups so early in the day?"

"I can hold my liquor, thank you very mush."

"Obviously not." Samuel grimaced. "Dear cousin, will you please see to Miss Bartlett? I'm afraid Zachary's given her a fright." He nodded to me. "Do forgive him, he isn't himself."

Who exactly is he, I wondered.

Zachary grumbled. "You shouldn't have given it to me, then, brother."

"Shut up. You need coffee."

"Pot calls the kettle black, you know."

Mr. Carter gave me his arm as they wandered off. "You're trembling. Are you alright?"

"I am now. Thank you." I swallowed against the sudden fear that had gripped me in coarse human form. "Good thing you came when you did—who knows what he might have done?"

"Samuel is afraid he'll say something incriminating. And he might have if we hadn't been close by." He looked around. "Where is Tessa?"

"I don't know. I was in a hurry to find you after my tea with Cecily." My stomach sickened. "She saw us—."

Mr. Carter smiled. "Act naturally, Miss Bartlett. My uncle approaches."

His tall form stopped before us, the silver of his hair glinting in the sun. "I don't know what's come over Zachary." He shrugged. "He rarely imbibes during the day, and even then, he would rather keep his wits." He plucked my hand from Mr. Carter's arm and placed it within the crook of his arm as affectionately as Grandfather. "Do forgive him, my dear."

"Of course." I was sure the smile I offered him was of the pitiful, shaky sort. I was not accustomed to being manhandled.

"Tell me, how was your tea with Cecily?"

I glanced back at Mr. Carter who gave a slight nod.

"Her rooms are...ravishing." I struggled for something to say so as to not offend. "Any young girl should appreciate them.

She is so well-trained!" What else could I say? That I'd been threatened with exposure and scandal? I daresay he might have agreed with his daughter's underhanded tactics.

Anything to gain the Bartlett fortune. I cringed from his touch. From his sons and his house.

A bumblebee flew by my ear and landed on Mr. Chinworth's face. He released me and swatted at the creature, but not before it stung my host directly on his cheek. He shouted and swore as I'd never before heard on the streets of London.

Mr. Carter ran to assist, along with a footman and his manservant. Instantaneous swelling changed his features as his uncharacteristic shouts continued.

Mr. Carter whispered to me in the mayhem of the moment. "God's justice, perhaps? I fear he desires your inheritance as much as any gent among the Ton." He leaned closer. "Meet me in the small parlor by the library."

I waited half an hour, pacing before the cold fireplace where we'd enjoyed toasting bread days ago. The promise of friendship in the offing.

Finally, he appeared with Tessa. She stayed in the adjacent library, perusing books. Giving us privacy?

"Keep her with you at all times, Emma."

He used my name again. I liked the sound.

"I must confess more to you." He glanced at Tessa, then me. "She is more to me than a hired maid."

More to him? How much more? I don't know why my spirit sank. I had no claim on him besides his valiant promise to my mother...

"She is my sister."

I lifted my eyes. "Your sister?"

"My step-sister to be exact. My father married her mother after my own mum's death. I'm sorry I kept it from you."

"I don't understand." My heart fluttered all the same. "Mr. Chinworth?"

"Doesn't know of her existence." He continued. "Tessa found herself widowed at a fairly young age." He pulled me down to sit beside him on the settee. "She needed something to keep herself busy." He shrugged.

"And you wanted to be certain of my happiness?"

"And safety."

"Until now, I've had neither concern nor much of an exciting life."

"True, your grandfather left no possibility of danger ever reaching a hair on your head."

I'd been so very isolated.

"Tessa is also trained to protect you if need be."

"Protect?"

"Zachary would be nursing a worse wound than his pride if Tessa had been by your side." A smile lifted the corners of his mouth.

"I've never heard of a lady who could defend herself."

"While men have their strength to recommend them, women are also strong. You can also protect yourself if need be." He nodded to Tessa who made her way to us. "I trained her myself after she endured an unsavory incident in London."

"Yes, brother." She smiled at me with compassion.

"Zachary had you in a lock hold. Who knows what he would have done if we hadn't come along."

My face burned.

"Watch, Emma." He took Tessa by the arm as I'd been taken. In a flash, she twisted out of his grip and had Mr. Carter on his knees.

"Oh!" What a strange sight! Women did not fight like common sailors but I did not desire to be accosted again without knowing what to do.

"I am not hurt, do not distress yourself." He stood. "I didn't think my cousins would become aggressive, but after what has happened, I need to be certain that you can ward them off. Neither of us plans to leave your side if we can help it, so I don't think you'll have that problem again. But I would feel better if you knew how to get the advantage, should the occasion arise and we are, for some reason, not directly at hand."

How did one protect against conniving little girls? Another problem for sure.

"Now watch us again. We will move slowly so you can see what's happening."

They performed the same act three more times.

"Your turn." Mr. Carter took my arm, and no matter what I did, I couldn't wrestle free from his grip. The scrapes from Zachary still stung.

He lifted his fist. "See the gap between my fingers? You'll want to throw your wrist out of my grasp from there. It is my weakest place."

I twisted and pulled. It worked.

We practiced again, and again. I felt like a rugged sailor, moving my body in such a forceful manner.

After the last round, Mr. Carter held my scraped, red wrist in his hands. "I am sorry." His gaze held mine again. So tender and caring. Where had Tessa gone? Was she in the library?

"Now, what were you going to tell me about Cecily?"

I relayed our conversation as his face paled.

"I should have been more careful."

"You couldn't have known..."

"Should I trust that she'll make good on her threat?"

He didn't answer but ran fingers through his fine, brown hair. "Are you certain she didn't hear what we spoke of?"

"Almost. I believe she spied us from a distance."

"Your options are to choose Samuel quickly or live down scandal for the rest of your life by marrying me. Which is it?" His lips quirked.

"I would take the second option, but—" I realized what I'd intimated. Embarrassment flooded. I had to fix my words somehow. "You would be a far safer option."

He winked. "Poor Zachary and Tobias left out of the equation, then?"

"Utterly."

"Hmm."

"When does her threat pay off?"

"By sundown, Saturday."

He looked up to the ceiling. "Four days to find Samuel's wife and child, see them to safety, and get you out of here, scandal-free." He looked back down at my face. "Pray, Emma, that we can do this quickly before anyone else gets hurt."

"Sometimes I wish I weren't an heiress."

His hand alighted beneath my chin as it had last night. "God will help you bear it."

Yes. I knew God would. But would Mr. Carter be around when this was over? Did he wonder the same?

He bent over my sore wrist and kissed the trail of scratch marks... "One day soon, Emma, you will dip your toes in the ocean. I know it." His lips lifted in a half-smile, then he strode from the room.

Dinner was a somber affair. Only Tobias and Mr. Carter were present and little conversation to be had, I left for my rooms. There was much I wanted to ask Tessa.

When had her mother married into Mr. Carter's family? Did she know my parents like her brother did?

More than ever, a desire to see their likeness increased.

When I opened the door to my room, there lay on a little silver salver, a folded bit of pink foolscap, sealed with wax. I lifted the seal to read: *Remember our agreement.*

God forgive me, but I'd hoped by sundown on Saturday that Cecily would be drugged into a stupor to keep from this rash behavior.

No. I knew that was the wrong desire. I swallowed down my fear. If I had to, I would marry Joseph Carter. Despite his not truly wanting such an outcome. But I knew as well as he that such measures wouldn't need to be taken. After all, his obligations to my safekeeping only went so far.

The mere idea of marrying him joined my simple but impossible dreams. Could he be the one? I'd not known many men. But I'd read extensively and did believe I'd seen enough of them, despite my lack of seasons. Joseph was a rare one. And undoubtedly out of my reach.

I felt his absence each time we parted. Berated myself for caring too much for a man who was doing what any true gentleman might. And yet...hope glimmered.

I stood in front of the fire in my private sitting room when Tessa joined me. "Your ruse has worked, my lady. They believe you have forgotten your intention to leave."

Oh, but I couldn't wait.

Tessa nodded with a smile. "We will hold out a little longer, yes?"

I nodded. "Please call me Emma. If we are to be friends."

She agreed. I asked her if she'd known my parents as her brother had.

"No. I wish I had, for your sake." She placed a kind hand between my shoulder blades. "I know Joseph will tell you what he can. All you need to do is ask."

"Perhaps when this is over..." For now, I needed to focus on surviving Mayfield Manor.

"We should pray for Joseph's success. He goes out tonight to look for Samuel's wife."

I prayed indeed. The whole night through, despite my exhaustion. My attempt at escaping and Joseph's gentle capture had propelled me into an entirely different objective.

When I saw him next, he shook his head. He hadn't been able to find her.

Three more days.

I'd forgotten to share my suspicions about Grandfather's medicine. Surely no one could be that evil—but then anything seemed possible with this family. Samuel's wife and Grandfather, regardless of station, were both precious in the sight of God.

Had my uncles conspired with Mr. Chinworth to force my choice so quickly? Seemed so. I was certain Uncle Richard and Gerald held no animosity towards Grandfather. No. They loved him and looked up to him. Yet I never expected to hear what Uncle Richard said as I was leaving either. Could it be true? Could they have conspired with Chinworth to see me inherit early so that one of his sons could take control all the sooner? Could they have helped Grandfather to his death? No. Surely not.

Tears threatened. My imagination had gone wild. With each outlandish, unexpected event, they morphed into bigger beasts. I had less to fear than supposed. Mr. Carter and Tessa would see me safely away. All would be well.

But Samuel's threat pressed by day's light. Would that I could drop the whole of my fortune into their greedy laps—for that is what they wanted—and run.

That would certainly be the simplest course.

Chapter Thirteen

I tried to keep my distance from Zachary the next morning, but he tracked his way towards me at the breakfast buffet. I tried to dodge him. He cornered me by the sausage platter.

"Miss Bartlett, I beg you to give me a moment of your time." His pained smile disgusted me.

"My last experience was less than enjoyable." Could I be any clearer?

A throat cleared from the table. Samuel's?

"I *will* have your forgiveness."

A demand then. I blinked slowly. "I would have my breakfast if you don't mind." Forgiveness, while given, should never be manipulated.

He swore under his breath. That mouth. Had the others heard?

Mr. Carter stood as I took my seat. "I have an announcement to make." He smiled at me. "As you know, Miss Bartlett has had little diversion besides time with us since arriving at Mayfield."

Samuel feigned sympathy.

Tobias nodded. "A shame, that."

"Uncle, realizing he can't be of service to you, Emma, thinks you could do with a small party today. One that might help you have respite from your mourning."

A party? When so much was at stake? What was he thinking?

"He has invited the Sherbornes to come here instead our going to Goodwyn Abbey. For a little ballroom dueling, if you will. We shall challenge each other in fencing, and the ladies will be our fair maidens attending. Not to mention my student needs to see what he is to learn. And you, my stalwart cousins, are prime examples."

Zachary sputtered. "You'll strike me in the first minute."

Samuel laughed, pointing. "Miss Bartlett, I warn you, don't tie your ribbon around his foil. He's no Lancelot."

"Matthew needs to see several examples of good swordsmanship." Joseph countered.

Samuel laughed louder, "I wouldn't call Zachary a *good* swordsman."

Tobias joined in. "He can sit with the ladies."

Zachary slapped the table with his hand. "Give me a pistol any day."

Mr. Carter flicked his gaze to me, then back to Zachary. "All in good fun. This isn't meant to be a real challenge. And think of what service you'll be to Matthew."

"A rags to riches story always warms the heart." Samuel laughed again before winking at me. "The young gentleman didn't know what was coming."

Tobias tossed his napkin on the table. "Is it true that he's been recovering from broken legs and an arm?"

Mr. Carter nodded. "Yes. He has made great progress, however."

"Must've got into some kind of scuffle." Samuel nodded. "I'm sure he'll reward you handsomely for your efforts. Wyndhouse could use the...investment."

Mr. Carter didn't sway at the offense. "Wyndhouse is perfect the way it is, thank you."

Zachary rolled his eyes. "Every man's home is his castle."

I'd been curious since I first heard of Wyndhouse. How close was it to my parent's home? They'd been neighbors.

"Lord Sherborne," Samuel worked a bit of ham from between his teeth, "made sure of his alliance with the boy by marrying his cousin, poor mouse though she was when he took her in." He took a bite of scone and chewed. "I have to hand it to him, the man knows when to gamble and when to hold. Lucky fellow."

The Sherbornes sounded like the wealthiest of families, ever eager for more. But Mr. Carter seemed to like them. Perhaps there was more to the story.

"I'm sure Lord Sherborne didn't know of the boy's parentage when he married Lady Sherborne." He smiled. "Indeed, what was a marriage of convenience turned out to be quite the love match." Mr. Carter pulled my chair and I stood. "We reconvene in three hours' time when the Sherbornes shall arrive."

The brothers scurried out, a challenge in their faces.

Mr. Carter turned to me. "I have business to attend to, please excuse me." His eyes spoke clearly. "We must talk before the Sherborne's arrive."

We had but two days. Two days before Cecily made good on her threat. Could she really do so much damage? Most possibly. Unwitting plans joining upon bigger unknown schemes.

Before I knew what I was doing, I made my way to Cecily's room. Her situation and behavior confounded me. I had so much compassion for the child, yet the danger that lurked—oh. God forgive her, she didn't know what she was doing.

I opened the door to the sickly-sweet pink rooms. The shades were drawn, little light filtered within.

Her nurse sat, fast asleep in a rocking chair by her side. An old, dour-looking woman. Had she been a good companion? I went to the other side of the bed where Cecily lay, her hands spread neatly at her sides, blankets up to her chin despite the warmth of the morning.

I gazed upon her flushed cheeks and the sweep of her eyelashes against creamy skin. Her angelic hair ran like a river over her pillow. Her breathing was slow and deep.

A sleeping beauty who needed to wake to the better things in life. Things I was only beginning to reach for and grasp. Would that I could take her with me and we might make these discoveries together.

I prayed for her once again and when I rose, I noticed a small bottle, half full. Just like the one Grandfather had used when suffering from gout. I picked it up and looked at the markings on the label. *G.W. Apothecary.*

Identical, I was sure of it.

Had Mr. Carter given it to him? No. I refused to entertain the idea. So unlikely considering everything else. Including his smile. How strange though, that the same bottle of medicine should be here as each apothecary prepared his own elixirs.

I placed the bottle back on the table and made my way out of the room. Neither Cecily nor the nurse awoke.

It was entirely possible that Mr. Chinworth knew of Grandfather's ailment and sent along his favorite cure. A kindness meant to kill? Had it killed him? And would it also end Samuel's suffering wife?

I went back inside the room, intent on taking the bottle to show Mr. Carter.

But the nurse had woken.

"What can I do for you, Miss Bartlett? You see, Miss Chinworth had a difficult night and is asleep, and will be abed for most of the day."

"I am sorry to hear it."

The nurse looked with compassion upon the sleeping child. "She don't know she's suffering when she goes into one of her fits, mind you. Goes out of her mind and doesn't remember a thing when she comes to." She nodded. "'Tis a blessing."

"And the medicine helps?"

"Keeps the fits away. Another blessing."

"I see. I won't keep you." I left the room, concern growing. Saturday night might very well come and go without her rousing. But I very much doubted it. The intensity of her threat begged notice. Did Mr. Carter know his young cousin well enough to realize that she wasn't committing a prank?

When I entered my private parlor, Mr. Carter and Tessa were there waiting for me.

Tessa smiled. "It's time for your next lesson."

Mr. Carter's arms drew around my waist without warning. "Now try to get loose."

I gasped at the feel of his strength. A sense of protection, not fear, muddied my thoughts. I recovered my senses and struggled against his hold. It was impossible. I couldn't free myself. Of course, I couldn't. Didn't truly want to.

He loosened his hold, but I didn't move, his own arms stalled.

Tessa cleared her throat.

My voice rasped. "I see your point, Mr. Carter. Show me what to do."

He nodded. "As I said, every woman should learn how to defend herself."

I quite agreed. Time to focus.

Tessa pushed my shoulders down and pulled my elbow up. "Bend at your waist—makes it hard to control you, move you. Then strike his face with your elbow like so, and a swift kick right..."

The remedy made me blush to kingdom come.

Before we were through, I'd doubled over laughing with Tessa while Joseph stood with his hands on his hips.

He winked at me. "One day, I will indeed show you how to use a pistol. You too, Tessa."

He was so very handsome and so very good. I could think of no scenario where I might wish to harm him. Or he me.

"Leave us, Joseph. We must dress for the Sherborne's arrival."

"In a moment." He waved me to where he stood to talk privately. "If you can muster the nerve, try to act as though you prefer Samuel today. Allow him to think that you regard him over the others. Lord Sherborne and I believe your positive regard will force his hand. We're confident he will go to his wife and we will follow him." He looked at the mantel clock coming upon the hour. "I only hope we aren't too late."

"What does Lord Sherborne know of my troubles?"

He lifted a hand and caressed the side of my face. "He is the best of men, Emma. I trust him with my life."

I swallowed, his tender touch sinking into my soul. "As I trust you."

His eyes flicked to my lips and then eyes. "I'm most grateful that you aren't the spoiled, petulant heiress I expected. I only meant to see you safely out of harm's way..." his voice trailed off. The clock chimed, and he drew away.

The day's activities would center around Samuel. My encouragement to force his hand—I shuddered at the thought of even giving the evil gentleman a smile. Doing more than that seemed very wrong. How could he hold his wife at so little value? Did she feel abandoned already? How had he convinced her to keep their marriage a secret? Many mysteries to ponder.

If I were truly in love and married, I'd want the world to know it. My attraction to Mr. Carter—Joseph—grew with each passing day. I couldn't deny it.

But was his heart mine? I could tempt the man with my fortune. 'Twould be easy. As good and upright as he seemed, would he withstand the temptation? Would he, like the others, marry me for the sake of preserving his own estate? To raise his fortunes, his position in society?

The harder question rose to the surface. Could he love me without it? I rolled my eyes at the ceiling. Such a droll thought. Grandfather's fortune chained me to its service. Like a dragon guarding its hoard.

But for what? What value did it have sitting there, protected? Did humankind work as a slave to gold, or did gold work for humankind?

Another item to discuss with my solicitor when this was over. How to shift the hoard from stagnancy to usefulness. I did not desire to be a trapped caretaker. Controlled by my fortune. Such seemed a weak kind of power.

Another thought slipped into my mind like an unwelcome splinter. Would my fortune stop Joseph from presuming to court me? I felt like a queen on the chess board. Always under attack. How did a woman let a gentleman know that she didn't consider herself above him? Especially when she admired everything about him.

Except, of course, his wealth. That had absolutely nothing to do with the equation.

CHAPTER FOURTEEN

A violent storm followed the Sherborne's arrival. Blinding sheets of rain swept across the estate with a vengeance. We stood before large ballroom windows and watched as the world changed from a peaceful spring tide to a dangerous new season— if anyone was brave enough to attempt to stand against its unbridled fury.

Thunder boomed and rattled the glass.

A cry sounded from the corner of the room. The man called Matthew sat huddled by the fireplace, shivering as though doused by the storm's icy fingers. His aunt, Lady Sherborne, crouched before him. The young man took a deep breath and slowly stood up.

His doctor gave a great laugh. "Well done, Master Dawes!" He clapped. "Next time you'll be able to stand at the windows with the rest of us."

The boy smiled weakly. "I would do so now if you will help me."

Lightening shimmered with the candle glow as Lord Sherborne and Dr. Rillian, as he'd been introduced, helped him.

Dr. Rillian turned and offered me a smile. "Yes, indeed. We must face many storms in life. It is best done with friends on either side of us. Wouldn't you agree, Miss Bartlett?"

"You're a poet, old man." Samuel laughed.

I nodded to him, not daring to look at Joseph and Tessa. Friends I had longed for, now appearing when I needed them the most.

As young Matthew reached the window, a loud crack, then a crash sounded nearby. His trembling increased. "Steady, now." The old doctor wrapped an arm around his back for support but the sound of breaking glass sent the boy to his knees.

Samuel swore and dashed from the room, Zachary after him.

Poor Matthew. What made him fear so? Terror shone in his eyes.

Tobias sidled near me. "It'll be the old tree by the solarium, I shouldn't wonder." He whispered into my ear. "Stay away from Samuel, if you know what's good for you." His eyes shifted. "A kind warning, Miss Bartlett. That is all."

I expected the brothers to warn me off, one from the other, as they vied for my hand. Truly, I would heed every warning given from now on. Did Tobias truly care? Doubtful, but I could not avoid Samuel today as I wished. I must help preserve the life of Samuel's wife. Tobias offered me his arm and I took it as he led me to a row of chairs where Lady Sherborne and I were to admire the men.

Lady Sherborne offered a congenial smile. "Please, call me Elaina."

"Very well." I wondered at this woman who had been forced into a marriage of convenience but seemed happier than anyone I'd ever met. However did she manage that feat?

Thankfully, the thunder soon rolled into the distance and the rain eased.

Elaina explained. "Matthew survived a shipwreck—and more. It will take him a while to adjust to his terrible memories."

I couldn't imagine surviving a sinking ship. "How awful."

"Yes. It was." Her eyes briefly fluttered.

Samuel reentered the room, Cecily trailing behind. She glanced at me, nose high —much like Mrs. Norris in London. I held back a laugh and smiled sweetly.

Time to flirt with Samuel. I hid a cringe, rose from my seat, and walked over. I curtsied. "I shall enjoy watching you defeat all your opponents."

"Well now." His lips slowly raised into an upward curve. He took my hand and kissed it. "I'm sure you shall."

I pretended to be pleased.

"As will I." Cecily tramped to the chair I'd vacated, a victorious smile on her face.

Samuel's eyes narrowed. "I hope, my dear, that you will not be disappointed."

"How could I be?" My own words sounded sickly sweet. I'd never practiced flirtations and was far from genuine. But I knew he didn't really care about my feelings, not as long as he won fair fortune.

He led me back to the ladies' seats with a bow and joined the men tying on protective clothing. Jackets had been tossed aside.

We watched the men spar in rounds, one after the other. I confess, my heart pounded at the sight of Joseph expertly wielding his foil. Even my untrained eye could tell he was the only proficient fencer in the room.

Matthew watched, entranced, laughing when Lord Sherborne nearly had Joseph cornered.

Zachary, as predicted, withdrew early. Scowling, he stood in the corner drinking a cup of tea, looking as though he wished for something stronger. Tobias was a fair sport but failed to hold position against Samuel.

I applauded and sent the man smiles as he cast his glances in my direction. His confidence grew and now, he and Lord Sherborne finally faced off.

A tea cart had been wheeled before us, Elaina did the honors of serving. Cecily sat biting her nails, refusing tea, until, in a swift motion, she ran to Samuel. She looked at me, drew him to the corner, and whispered in his ear.

His body stilled. He glanced at Joseph, then, gazed at me. His look lingered. I stared into my cup as dread filled my stomach. She'd told him. The little sneak.

The ferocity with which he sparred against Joseph troubled me. Even Lord Sherborne tensed. His brothers closed in, their arms folded.

Joseph shouted, "Halt!"

But Samuel refused. He continued to clash and thrust until Zachary and Tobias shouted at him.

"Halt, for goodness' sake. Are you trying to kill him?"

"Perhaps." Samuel laughed. "Unlike the rest of you, Joseph can handle a real fight."

Joseph removed his protective mask as sweat trickled down his face. "A real fight? Are we not here to school Master Dawes?" He wiped his face with a handkerchief. "You wield the foil as a rapier at war."

Samuel smirked. "Rapier, saber, blunt foil—what does it matter? I knew you could handle the fight, cousin." He bowed to us, winked at me, then said, "I believe it is time for luncheon."

He and his brothers left the room, and our guests were led away to freshen up. I wanted to talk to Joseph, but Cecily hung about like a buzzing fly. So instead, I escaped to my room where Tessa waited with a message.

You're doing great. Keep it up. –J

I folded it against my heart. Soon. So very soon, this would all be over.

At luncheon, Samuel rapped his spoon upon his crystal water glass. "I quite agree with Joseph. Miss Bartlett deserves more engagement. Which is why I have accepted the invitation to the Butterton Hall Ball on everyone's behalf. Tomorrow night, it is. What say you all?"

He grinned at me as though he'd handed me heaven, as if placating a childish female.

"I'm not sure—would it be appropriate? My grandfather's death...and me still in mourning."

He brushed my words away with his hand. "I assure you that no one will signify it. In fact, not enough people in society will even recognize you as Lady Bartlett. They think you're hidden away at Chatswick with your uncles, I shouldn't wonder."

Joseph chimed in. "A ball would do you good, I think."

He approved. To what end? "Will you be in attendance, Lady Sherborne?"

She nodded. "Zander and I are expected."

I looked at Samuel as boldly as I dared. "As long as you will offer your hand for my first dance, Mr. Chinworth."

His eyes narrowed. "I won't dance with anyone else, Miss Bartlett."

Surely, he didn't mean each and every dance. Idle tongues would wag. Even I knew this wasn't done. Would be scandalous!

Tomorrow was Saturday. If we were to force his hand and see me safely away from Mayfield, it had to happen tonight. Lord Sherborne and Mr. Carter simply must find Samuel's wife and child.

I spent the remainder of the day giving the man most of my attention. He laughed more, grew more confident with each passing hour. All that remained was the offer he expected me to make, as my backward grandfather had promised of me.

Elaina had been playing the pianoforte when a message was delivered to Samuel. He withdrew to the window to read it in the waning sunlight. He let out a breath and pocketed the note, making a beeline for me.

He took my hands and dared to touch where a wedding ring might reside. His expression carried the meaning. What had Cecily told him exactly? I supposed it didn't matter if all she sought to do was make him jealous and frighten me at the same time. At both tasks, she seemed to have succeeded.

I'd made my presumed preferences clear this day. I yawned behind my hand, anxious to get this day over with. "I have a headache—I do believe I shall retire for the night."

The gentlemen stood, and Elaina moved from the instrument. "So wonderful to meet you, Emma. I hope I get the chance to enjoy your company again" She curtsied. "I will see you tomorrow night, then."

Samuel smiled. "You may get your wish to see her as often as you like, Lady Sherborne. Perhaps sooner than expected."

I forced a bright smile and exited the room, nearly running all the way to my quarters. I thrust the door shut and slipped the lock into place. Tessa dropped her book and came to my side.

"I couldn't bear another moment of his attention." My head truly was pounding.

"Come. All will be well."

How long until Samuel crept from the estate to commit his evil deed? How long until Joseph and Lord Sherborne caught him red-handed? Hours. Mere hours. Then I would be free. I readied for bed, not sure that I could gain rest as Tessa adamantly recommended. Somehow, amid the anxiousness of the hour, I slept.

A hand shook me awake. Tessa? Candlelight glowed about her face, her mop cap and gown as bright as a ghostly moon.

"I have news," she whispered, her expression pained.

I sat up, a nervous pit in my stomach. I'd hardly been able to eat at supper.

She shook her head. "Samuel's wife..." Her face screwed with worry, "She died, Emma."

"He killed her?" My hands clasped tightly against my mouth. The monster.

"No—no, he didn't. Samuel didn't have to. She died of natural causes. An attending physician was with her the entire time."

I could scarcely think through the implications. "And the child? Did they find his child?"

Tessa nodded. "The boy is gone with his mother. The same illness afflicted two souls. Joseph was told it was cholera. From dirty water."

No crime, except for the fact that his wife and child had been denied their rightful places here at Mayfield. They would have survived had they been allowed better living conditions. Of this, I had no doubt.

Joseph and Lord Sherborne's attempt to stop Samuel and hold him accountable had been in vain. At least the poor woman would never know of his nefarious thoughts. I grieved for so young a life gone from this earth. Yet I could trust the same loving God who held my parents in His hands, also held her and her infant son.

"Joseph says we will make a new plan tomorrow."

I would not come out of my rooms tomorrow. Not if I could help it. Dear God, the poor woman and child...

If at all possible, I would make my exit before the ball. Yes. Indeed, this must be my plan.

After yesterday's events, every moment seemed to move slowly. I didn't go down to breakfast. Tessa ordered a tray. I would start packing as soon as I was dressed. My purpose at Mayfield Manor was at an end. What could Cecily do to me besides create an embarrassment?

I didn't want to find out.

Chapter Fifteen

Cecily, uninvited, visited my parlor. How I wished Tessa hadn't left the room.

"Papa's allowing me to attend the ball, so I'll be watching you when a certain announcement is made." Her posture reminded me of her father's. Ramrod straight, high chin, to be obeyed.

If all went as planned, I wouldn't be anywhere near Butterton Hall by then. "Have you made your debut into society already?" She couldn't be more than twelve years of age.

She rolled her eyes. "The people of Butterton don't care about such details." She spotted the corner of my trunk from beyond the doorway. "That's strange. You aren't leaving?"

"Doing a bit of organizing." I smiled, hoping to allay her suspicion.

"Interesting." Her slippered toe circled a pattern on the rug. "I'd hate to think how devastated you'd be to end up with my poor cousin."

My heart lunged. One might use a stronger word than "devastated..."

"I see the idea upsets you." Her hands were folded tightly, knuckles white.

I turned my head just so, as I'd seen my governess do when she saw into the tender heart of my childish behavior. "How lovely it would be to enjoy the company of a girl like you, day after day."

Her chin jerked, her eyes questioned.

"I know how you must feel living in a house full of men. Only men. Must be trying to find decent feminine company." I sent her my warmest smile. "Did you know that I was raised by my grandfather and uncles?"

Her lips parted and her back relaxed against the cushion, her hands unknotted, one hand stroking her long, silken braid. Both of us bereft of a mother's love. If it weren't for Mrs. Grayson's especial care, I'm not certain I would know what friendship was well enough to long for it as I did.

Tessa returned, carrying my recently laundered shawl. "Good morning, Miss Chinworth." She placed it about my shoulders. "Quite chilly today."

Cecily's nurse barged through my door, her brows knit, her patience tried. "You can't run from me, dear. It's time for your medicine!"

"I shall not sleep today." Cecily's voice bit and clipped once again

I tightened my shawl about me. "Is she not attending the ball?"

The nurse laughed. "Whatever gave you that idea?" She tugged the girl out of her seat. "You've not been fibbing to Miss Bartlett, have you?"

"I know Papa will let me attend. All I need to do is ask. He lets me do whatever I want."

"Not tonight, missy."

Cecily turned a pained expression toward me as she was led through the door, back to her rooms. Forced to sleep with that awful elixir?

Joseph arrived soon after luncheon. I had been growing anxious for an answer to my query. *When, oh when, could I leave?* I couldn't bear these circumstances much longer.

Weariness hung around him like a cloak, dark circles beneath his eyes spoke of the long night he'd endured. The fire crackled in the quiet. "The child isn't dead as we thought. The doctor feared for his life and hid him with a trusted friend. For now, he has allowed Samuel to believe his son is deceased." He rubbed the scruff on his jaw. "He didn't lie to Samuel, mind you. Samuel made the assumption. So eager he's been to be rid of his family. Despicable."

"How does a mere babe threaten him?" I could not fathom that such a tiny, innocent life should have to be hidden from harm.

"As the firstborn son of a legal marriage—if it was indeed legal—he stands to inherit Mayfield. Why else would he desire her death? Were it not, he might have tossed her away without a second thought, as many before him have done."

Tessa motioned toward the chair by the fire. "You look tired. Sit down, Joseph."

He did as bidden and closed his eyes for a moment before looking at me. "I'd hoped to have you both away from here by now, but I must ask you to endure another night or two. Lord Sherborne has sent out men to search for marriage records. Samuel will certainly be found out soon."

"So I must attend the ball after all." A sigh escaped.

"Yes."

"And what if Cecily tells Mr. Chinworth?"

"I doubt Uncle would believe her tale, though true."

"Did you know that she is being drugged to keep from seizures?" Fear clutched my heart. "Joseph, she uses the same medicine that Grandfather used before he died. I recognized the bottle when I visited her. I suspect it's the same potion that trapped me upon my bed for days—and what Samuel thought to use to end his wife's life."

"I delivered a packet to your Grandfather when I retrieved you. From Uncle. I didn't know what was in it, but per-haps...Emma, I am terribly sorry. I wish I knew."

"How else would he have something from an apothecary far from home?"

Joseph blanched. "Then your grandfather's death may not have been entirely natural." He stood. "Enough. We leave now."

In that moment, I saw my escape to freedom, clear as the sky. Wide open. Only there was a child, trapped in her own tower. An innocent who needed our help. Who needed res-cue from whatever concoction they'd been dumping down her throat. And Samuel's baby—hidden away from unholy demise. I couldn't help him. But maybe I could help Cecily.

"Cecily..." A clog formed in my throat.

"You care for her, even after she threatened you?" He looked surprised.

"She doesn't know her right from her left." Poor thing.

"We cannot steal her away."

How I wished we could.

He took a deep breath. "I will meet with Uncle—see what I can find out about the miracle medicine...Where it's made..."

Tessa shook her head. "From what I hear, he is incoherent. A terrible reaction from the bee stings—and likely also being fed more of that elixir."

Joseph rolled his eyes. "Worse than an opium den. I wouldn't be surprised if that's what it is. Or some form of it." He took my hand. "Get through the day, Emma. Then I'm getting you out of here, no matter what. We'll attend the ball and go on as before—and pray that the Almighty will lend us a firm hand. Sherborne's men must find that marriage record."

"Tobias warned me away from Samuel yesterday. Perhaps he honestly cares for me, maybe even would help."

His brows rose. "He was aptly horrified by his brother's designs." He squeezed my hand. "You are right, he may. Much to do before tonight. Pray without ceasing, Emma."

"It is all I do these days."

Tessa rose. "I'll inquire about the medicine below stairs."

"Thank you."

The day waned. I need only endure one further afternoon and evening in this place. But what could I do for Cecily? The medicine may very well keep her from seizures. Did she sleep yet? I would go see.

I should have stayed in my rooms as planned. Samuel met me in the hallway, eyes no doubt red from lack of sleep rather than grief. He'd come from Cecily's room. In his hand, almost hidden was a small jar. He slipped the medicine into his pocket.

"You've missed the imp. She's already asleep." He leaned toward me but corrected himself when her nurse stepped through the door and shut it.

"Pardon me—didn't know you both were hovering so near."

Samuel moved out of her way with a measure of impatience. "Nurse."

I hurried behind the woman down the hall—but paused remembering to play my part. I sent a smile over my shoulder. "Looking forward to the ball?"

His expression turned as dark as his midnight black hair. "Passionately."

"Until then." I would have to dance with him. For my many years of longing to be out in society, I never imagined that for my first social dance, I'd be paired with such a man.

I caught up to the old woman. I would do my own digging. "Nurse?"

"Yes, Miss Bartlett?"

"When do you expect Cecily to wake?"

"Ah, she'll be sleepin' for hours yet. Come midnight, I'll give her another dose."

"What are her seizures like? The poor girl..."

The nurse looked about before answering. "I never seen a one, but I hear they're awful. Chinworth says it must be from my expert care." She placed a hand over her heart. "Love her like she were my own."

Hmmm...I wondered. "Seems a hard way to live—to do naught but sleep."

She cocked her head. "Oh, aye. Better than seizing, I'm sure. Good day, Miss." She curtsied and left.

She never saw a seizure? Not once? Impossible? Hadn't Mr. Chinworth mentioned that she'd had a bad night recently? And what did Samuel plan to do with the bottle he'd snatched? I wondered if Joseph's comparison to an opium den might be accurate. Could an apothecary truly create such a dangerous concoction?

I hied back to my room, back to the lakeside windows where I'd already spent much time in prayer. But this time, instead of asking for my own protection, I prayed for Cecily's. And hers alone.

As the May twilight glimmered its last, I took the hand of my would-be fiancé and stepped into the carriage. Tobias entered too—I wondered at the flash of irritation Samuel sent him. Then I realized that he intended for the two of us to be alone on the way to Butterton Hall. When Samuel wasn't looking, Tobias nodded at me, his lips drawing a serious line. He knew something. But did he seek to help – or hinder?

Zachary and Joseph rode behind us. The steady sound of hooves gave comfort. As trapped as I felt, Joseph wasn't far.

CHAPTER SIXTEEN

"Invite the Ton, did you?" Samuel shook Lord Camden's hand.

The crush of people had been unexpected. Where did they all come from? I curtsied to Lady Camden before taking Samuel's strong arm again. Joseph walked behind us. I drew a breath, anxious for this night to be over.

Butterton Hall glowed. Candles burned high and low, creating pools of light among the well-dressed. A path opened before us and eyes swept over me as we made our way deeper into the throng. Curiosity evident as always. Never had I been so openly observed within a crowd.

The urgency of Joseph and Lord Sherborne's mission pressed. They mustn't fail. "There is Elaina." I extricated my hand from his hold and made my way to her side. How glad I was to see someone who knew, who understood my struggles. If only a little. Her deep lavender gown fit the occasion, her simple jewelry and headdress rather underdone, compared to those preening around us. For a woman of her station, she did not flaunt wealth but exuded a quiet confidence.

She linked arms with me and shooed the men away. "Let me take my new friend around."

Samuel bowed, his eyes locking mine. "I shan't let you out of my sight, my dear."

I chilled against his entrapping words and turned to Elaina. "I confess, I've never attended a ball."

"Should you dance if asked?"

"Grandfather made sure I learned all of the dances." I laughed at the irony. "He never allowed me a season, however. I am a few years out of practice."

"Never a Season? I can't say you've missed anything important." She lent a knowing smile. "Be warned, Emma, it seems the cream of the Ton has descended upon Butterton. I know not how or why. Perhaps a certain someone let the cat out of the bag about a certain heiress..." She looked beyond me. Recognizing faces?

"Come to think of it, some of the guests have been watching me. I thought perhaps something was wrong with my blue silk..."

"Nothing at all, except your loveliness exceeds the manufactured beauty around us."

"Do you think they know who I am?"

"I'm sorry, Emma. They spoke of you openly, anticipating your arrival. You were London's best-kept secret and it appears they have gathered for your debut."

"They anticipated me because of my fortune."

"Isn't it despicable?"

Samuel's solemn assurances that no one would know my identity furthered my dislike of him. "How inappropriate I must appear. I should be wearing black and biding my time at home."

"You would only seem inappropriate should you be found to be penniless. No, indeed. They are too curious and too anxious to be linked to someone of your importance." She patted my hand. "I am so very sorry. Soon, you will have a chance to grieve without worrying about others. I, too, have been through such times."

I held back the sudden threat of tears. How many I'd choked back already! I'd never known a day without Grandfather. And now I'd never see him again.

We approached Lord Sherborne, who bowed. "Good evening, Lady Bartlett. I see you found my bride."

Elaina blushed under his regard before turning to me. "The first dance begins in a few minutes. Whatever happens, Emma, you have friends." Her voice lowered to a whisper. "We will help you."

The ball would last for hours, I'd been told. Would that time fly as the old Latin expression bespoke.

Samuel took my hand and led me to the floor. His touch repulsed. For the sake of his innocent child, I allowed it. I kept thinking about the poor baby while barely managing the steps of a simple quadrille.

I danced and turned and faced my partner, again, wondering how this father could be so callous to his child's welfare. The man's core was selfishness. So unlike his cousin... Joseph.

I heard my title *Lady Bartlett* bandied about, much like I had walking to the churchyard in London. Prying eyes, prying ears. Prying hands that would take a fortune and not a heart. Thieves, all. The music stopped, I curtsied, and the beast bowed before leading me off the floor.

A couple begged for introductions, and they were made. All sought the honor of my acquaintance. Samuel beamed and pulled me to the dance floor again. The second dance. I had not thought one could pray to God during a set and yet I did. Psalm 91, the vicar had whispered to me on that Sunday. So long as I danced within His shadow—I need not fear.

Eventually, a few other men came to claim my hand. Samuel leaned close before releasing me to Sir Thomas. "Rest assured, we will dance a third..." The implications were clear. Another wan smile to encourage.

Anything but another dance.

I looked for Elaina, nowhere to be seen. Where was Joseph? If only he were the one asking for me. If only the room emptied to all but true friends. I tried to find them, only to have Samuel at my elbow. The doorways were blocked with guests. I panicked. Why hadn't Joseph asked me to dance? Seen after my welfare? How strange that they'd all but disappeared.

Samuel turned to speak to an acquaintance and I made for an opening. A man filled the space, and Samuel's hand wrapped around my arm. Hurting me. "This way to supper, Emma. Wouldn't want you to get lost now, would we?"

I had no choice but to follow.

Supper was a lavish affair. I could hardly eat for the knot in my stomach. The tables were crowded with guests and abundant floral arrangements of lilies and strawberries on the vine. Dessert, it was said, would be a surprise—hidden behind pocket doors beside the dining hall. I was miserable. And no sweet vain concoction would cure it.

Samuel tossed back his fifth glass of wine. I moved to rise from the table and seek a quiet corner, but his hand held me fast.

I gave him an encouraging smile. "Eager, Mr. Chinworth, to claim the third dance so soon?" Dancing had already recommenced. "I must to the lady's lounge."

He released me with a wide grin. "Come back quickly or I will have to find you." He stroked my hand while I withheld a deep cringe. "I'd hate for you to miss dessert." His eyes pinned mine with a meaning I couldn't decipher.

"I will not be far, I promise." I would make my way to the lady's lounge to sit and beg God for this night to be over. I left the roaring crowds to an empty hall on the other side of the ballroom.

I'd gone but a few steps when a pair of hands pulled me into a shadow of a room. A door closed behind me. Joseph.

"Emma." He was breathless. "We must hurry."

Crowds walked past and I could hear the music beginning again.

"Blast."

"What's wrong? Did they—"

That's when I noticed the room we were in. Clusters of candles glowed along a central table and above the hearth. A large cake sat in the middle in the shape of a castle. Strange and unexpected. Of course, the surprise dessert...

Lady Camden's voice rang from the other side of the pocket doors, just in front of the grandiose confection.

Joseph grabbed my hand and pulled me to the doors. "Forgive me, Emma." He wrapped an arm around my waist and placed his hand tenderly upon my face. "Samuel plans to ruin you this night. I won't let him."

The doors slowly slid open and Joseph's lips crashed upon mine in a lover's embrace. The applause that began in anticipation of the gaudy cake, died away to a silent pulse in my ears. My heart pounded. Eyes scorched me. My lips burning from shock, from fear, from desire.

He released me and faced the stunned crowd with my hand tucked tightly within his. "You may congratulate us if you will." His grip tightened, and my heart refused to slow down.

A few gloved hands clapped, while others murmured something about my being ruined. I could not face them. I didn't understand what was happening. What had Joseph said? That Samuel planned to ruin me himself? Samuel planned to ruin me. In front of the ton. But Joseph... What had he done?

Samuel roared and threw his wine glass at Joseph who ducked, the crash of crystal behind us. "You conniving beggar. I will kill you."

"Quickly." Joseph pulled me through the door as Samuel plunged after us. Zachary barred the way through the morning room, but Joseph drew a pistol from his coat and cocked the hammer.

"You won't get away with her," Zachary growled.

Joseph pushed me through the door. "Run."

He pulled me along—I ran as fast as I could—into the dark covering of trees behind Butterton Hall. A carriage waited.

Tobias stood by the door and opened it wide. "Go quickly, cousin. If he suspects I helped you, there'll be the devil to pay."

We lunged through the door and sped away. Joseph pointed the pistol away from us and slowly put the hammer down. He released a breath and put his arm around me as I panted.

A silver-topped walking stick glinted in the moonlight, a smiling face sat across from us. "Lord Sherborne?"

"Good work, Joseph Carter."

"I don't understand. What has happened? Why did you...?" My face still burned.

He took my hand and looked into my face with real sorrow. "Samuel set up guards around you all night. We couldn't get close until he and the others had enough to drink."

"Why would he do such a thing?"

Lord Sherborne grunted. "He was going to publicly ruin you before the entire ton, no less. The ruination would have given you no choice but to marry him." He clicked his teeth. "We had to work fast."

I shook my head. "I would never marry him. I still don't understand." One could be ruined in many ways. Being alone in a room with a man for a long period of time for instance.

Or—an unchaperoned embrace. Then I realized. Joseph had destroyed my reputation before Samuel could.

"We didn't have time, Emma. I'm sorry. Samuel's associates somehow knew to not let me near you."

"If I had tried to leave, then…"

"He wasn't going to let you. When you walked by, I had to take my only chance." Pink spots flushed his cheeks. "Did you drink the wine that was served?" Joseph seemed concerned.

"I dared not touch it, even there."

"I am glad to hear it. I believe he drugged your wine and was waiting for you to get drowsy. Forgive my crass speech, Emma. But he planned to—" He paused. "I cannot say it." He swallowed. "And we weren't sure that Tobias would follow through."

The bottle Samuel had placed in his pocket—he'd stolen it from Cecily's room. I swallowed fear as my heart picked up speed. "Such evil."

"He was determined to marry you, no matter what."

Lord Sherborne handed Joseph another pistol which he placed within a leather pouch. The carriage slowed. "Get out here, and meet the other carriage on the other side of town by dawn."

Joseph helped me down and we stepped into the cover of a dark wood. We quietly made our way through bramble, old leaves, and crackling twigs. Did they find the marriage contract? What about the baby?

After several minutes, Joseph stopped. "If I could change the course of events this night, I would have. For your sake, I desired your freedom, despite the way you've changed my heart in the last few weeks. Despite the fact that your hand fits just so in mine." He pressed my hand between both of his. "And that your dreams carry with them an anticipation that makes me want to carry them out for you. With you."

He slipped to one knee. "I do not seek your fortune, Emma, except the boundless fortune of your heart."

My fingers had woven with his, I knew not when. Tears gathered unbidden.

"I wish circumstances could be different, but know this. I desire to marry you—as we now must. Will you seek your adventures, with me by your side?"

I knelt beside him and sobbed into his chest. How deeply I'd craved his care. His regard. His love. He stroked my hair and murmured a prayer. He held me tightly until I calmed.

I looked into his eyes. He deserved an answer. "I desire this as well."

"Our night isn't over." He brushed tears away from my eyes with his thumbs. "The vicar awaits our arrival. We will say our vows in a few hours. We must indeed rush, my love. Samuel's threats grow by the minute, and news of our scandal will reach London papers by morning."

We picked our way through the village, hiding behind buildings as various people rode past. Looking for us? Me?

We made it to the vicar's back door. He quickly let us in.

He smiled wide and winked at me. "Ah, the lovebirds must flee. Well then. Come. My wife will see to your needs. Dawn draws near and the ceremony must take place at church."

The kind woman led me up the stairs and helped me wash my tear-stained face. "Do you love the gentleman, my dear?"

"More than I ever thought possible." The new admission sang in my heart even as danger harkened.

"You will bind yourself to him, for life." Her eyes wrinkled, amused, but desiring truth. "For life, mind you. Is this what you want? Your vows will be unbreakable."

I thought of everything Joseph had been for me. From the month prior—and as far back as his valiant behavior as a boy. This man cared for me—wanted to help me live a life outside of a tower. He'd protected me, taught me to protect myself.

Oh yes, I desired him. But did he truly desire me? He'd spoken beautiful things to me in the wood, when I'd wept. Good though he was, did he crave what every man did? Money? But that bare thought didn't fit. Not at all.

The vicar's wife smoothed my hair and placed a bundle of posies in my hands. "Every bride ought to have a bouquet." She took my free hand and prayed a quick prayer. "Lord, bless this young woman who loves You and seeks Your care and will for her life. Bless her union with Joseph. May their marriage be a testimony to the beauty and strength of Your church. Amen.

Bolstered by her words, I walked down the stairs.

Joseph waited for me. "There is something you should know before we speak vows." He looked at the vicar who nodded encouragement. "Before the ball, I received word from your Uncle Richard..."

"Yes?"

"I never wanted your fortune, Emma."

"You'll have it regardless." The thought stung. Not that he would have control of it, but that it was ever a factor in my life at all. But the idea that I might bless him with what I brought to the marriage made me smile. Previously, I'd only thought of it as a curse.

"I will have you for richer or poorer, Emma." His eyes burned into mine. "What I'm trying to tell you is that your fortune is—gone."

"Gone?" Breath left my lungs.

"There is little left."

"You speak the truth?" Questions fled as I thought of our love.

"I have his letter here. I will share it with you as soon as I can."

Samuel would have ruined me—then abandoned me to face the shame alone when he discovered I was no longer an heiress. He would have wrecked me—but for Joseph. If I had married him first, before the loss of my fortune...I shuddered to think. I would not have survived the year. My body and soul both would have been at risk.

"I truly own nothing?" My limbs grew weak at the knowledge.

"Yes, my dear pauper."

The vicar laughed. "We must hasten."

Joseph took my hand as we made our way to the church. Down a little stone pathway and through a set of arched doors.

As the sunrise peered through the stained glass windows, we spoke our vows to one another. He looked tenderly upon me, love in his eyes. I found no reason to doubt anything he'd said.

A ring slipped onto my finger, his lips found mine, a slow, warm caress, more gentle than the embrace that sealed our fate. He leaned his forehead against mine. I had no fortune but for the man before me, and, he alone held my heart.

We signed our names in the register, side by side.

"How did we manage to skip reading the bans?" Would we not have to run to Scotland?

"Lord Sherborne insisted I carry a special license to marry you—if worse came to worse. And it did."

The vicar's brow furrowed. "For better or worse, you two need to go. Swiftly now."

His wife handed me a satchel. "Food for your journey."

Our journey? To where?

Joseph took my hand as we stood on the threshold of the church. "Ready to live life together?"

"Yes."

His deep brown eyes smiled. "We're off then."

I held his arm as if I'd never let go.

CHAPTER SEVENTEEN

We traversed the village, as quietly as we could. Many families were already up and about chores or preparing for Sunday services. Doors creaked and slammed shut—breakfast scents filled the air.

The smells enticed me. I'd hardly eaten last night.

Joseph led me behind the livery stables and pointed. "Zachary—just there." He whispered.

I saw him. Craning his neck through the opening of the tack shed—searching for us? I dearly hoped we didn't have far to go.

"When I count to three, we're going to run. As fast as we can."

I nodded.

Before we could take a step, one of the wolfhounds bounded around the corner—I screamed amid shouting—Zachary's voice booming across the yard. He'd spotted us.

Joseph pulled me. "Quick, the carriage is just over the bend, behind the mill. You can't see it, but it will be waiting."

Freedom was in sight. So near.

"One...two...three..." We ran— Zachary shouted again. More voices joined his.

"Wait!" Was that Tessa? A flash of her cloak disappeared behind the stable. I turned to see Zachary sprinting, Samuel close behind. Each hand held a pistol. He lifted one, and with wobbly aim, fired—Zachary convulsed and fell hard upon the ground.

I screamed as another shot followed—there was a burn in my side, a stabbing punch to my leg. Joseph threw himself between me and the raging scream that followed. The carriage stood before us—pain tore at my waist, blood spreading, staining the blue silk of my gown. The world grew fuzzy.

"Emma!" Joseph yelled. His arms held me. Somehow, we were in the carriage.

He gently set me down as searing pain crept first across my stomach, then down my leg. It was too much. I feared for my life.

"Dear God, help me."

The carriage rushed down the rutted road as the anguish increased.

Joseph eased me onto the seat. "Lie flat." He pushed a folded handkerchief into the wound. "Press tightly. Whatever you do, don't let go."

He unwound his cravat and wrapped it tightly around the joint. Every breath burned. "Joseph." I felt faint.

"Hang on, dearest."

I focused on the ceiling, what else could I do to allay the pain? Joseph wrapped more cloth around my leg.

Where were we going? I needed help. Desperately. "Zachary..." Had he been killed? By shots intended for me? Why would Samuel want to murder me? I didn't understand...

"Hush, Emma. Stay still. Be very quiet." His gentle voice rumbled "I failed to protect you..."

His face became indistinct. When I woke, Joseph carried me. Urgent shouts rose. Pain, so much pain. Unendurable.

Voices I recognized flitted close by.

"Steady, dear girl." Doctor Rillian.

Joseph's hand took mine. "Doctor Rillian is going to help you."

Fabric ripped—my beautiful dress was cut away.

"Double barrels. Couldn't even aim—he was drunk, Doc." A sob arose from my husband's throat.

Someone momentarily placed a warm cloth over my eyes that smelled of lavender and chamomile. Fingers pushed and prodded at my waist—at my leg.

"Clean shot, praise God. No organs appear to be damaged. But we must get the bullet out."

Doctor Rillian's face hovered over mine. "I need to operate, lass. Can you be strong?"

I nodded. I had little choice.

"Here, drink this."

I hesitated. "No drugs, please."

"Ah. Whyever not?"

Joseph informed him. "Chinworth put opiates in her wine and tea. And likely drugged Cecily as well."

"Yes. I could see it in the child's eyes. Do trust me, Mrs. Carter. I mean you no harm. My drink will indeed make you drowsy, but I will not give it to you without your permission."

Joseph kissed my forehead. "You are safe here. I promise." His voice cracked and a tear dripped.

"Alright."

Joseph raised me enough to swallow. The burn across my stomach singed me again.

"Only enough to help you relax. There now. We're about to start."

The world tilted once more. A tightly wound piece of cotton was placed between my teeth. Joseph stroked my hair as the doctor began. He knelt, his face close to mine, speaking the loveliest of words. I couldn't comprehend them for the pain, but his voice carried me along the currents of rising and falling agony.

Tears ran like waterfalls. It was worth it, I decided, in the middle of that little hell. It was worth losing everything, worth running, worth being shot—to know the kind of love that Joseph gave me.

Next, Dr. Rillian cleaned my wounds and re-bandaged them. And then, I acquiesced to the use of laudanum. Anything to stifle the throbbing pain.

Joseph set a cot beside my bed and refused to leave my side.

Where were we? Oh yes. My beloved had brought us to Goodwyn Abbey. Lord Sherborne's home. Elaina...my friend would be there.

I awoke the next day to three smiling faces bending over me. Joseph, Doctor Rillian, and Elaina.

"My husband." I managed a weak smile.

"My wife." He grinned. "Rise and shine...though maybe you shouldn't rise quite yet."

"What time is it?"

"Just in time for luncheon."

Doctor Rillian held a tray with a bowl in his hands. "Broth. Nothing better."

I was hungry. So very hungry.

Broth only? "Might I have bread as well?"

"I suppose. But one piece only, mind you."

"What about the baby?"

Dr. Rillian stilled. "Baby? What? Why wasn't I made aware..."

Elaina stepped forward. "She means Mr. Samuel Chinworth's child, don't you dear?"

"Of course. Did they find the marriage contract?"

"Not yet."

"Did they catch him?" A memory rushed after me. Zachary being shot. His eyes, wide with shock. "Zachary..."

No one answered. Joseph took the cup of broth from the doctor, easing himself to my side. "Sip this and gain some strength. Then we will talk."

The others left the room. I knew it must be bad news. How devastating this would be for the Chinworth family. And for what? Was not life more precious than anything?

I obediently sipped the broth and took small grateful bites of bread. Was all I could manage. Though hunger roared like a lion, I'd grown so very weak.

"Zachary didn't survive, Emma." His voice grew tight. "And Samuel is missing."

"Was it he that killed him?" And shot at me?

"Yes. Witnesses are willing to testify." He lifted my fingers to his lips and kissed them. "My love, you suffer for my sake. He'd been aiming at me, seeking revenge for taking you from him. He meant to kill me, not Zachary. Not you."

"He had too much to drink at supper."

"A dangerous combination, weapons and wine." He kept my hand close to his face. "There is more. My uncle is near death's door. An empty bottle of Cecily's elixir was found at his bedside."

"Mr. Chinworth?" I swallowed at the implications.

"Lord Sherborne and I suspect that Samuel wasn't merely anxious to get at your fortune. He was anxious to gain full control of what he had coming to him."

"By forcing himself upon me and killing his father, as he'd thought to do to his wife..."

"I'm afraid so."

"I should have listened to you when you warned me in London." It seemed like a lifetime ago.

"You were accustomed to doing what was expected of you, I do not fault that." He kissed my palm. "I should have been a better protector."

I looked at his handsome face, kind eyes, and scruffy jaw. "I daresay any adventure comes with a risk. I couldn't stay in my locked tower a moment longer. Wasn't your fault, Joseph." Truly, it wasn't. "You couldn't know the depths to which Samuel had fallen."

"You're right on that point."

"And we are married." I couldn't hide my delight.

His lips flicked a smile. "Now there's a state I didn't see coming. At least not so soon." He laughed. "Lord Sherborne was wise to suggest I be prepared."

"Are you sorry?"

"Only for your sake. For mine," he leaned over and pressed another kiss to my forehead, "I am entirely selfish."

"I think we would both be well to leave off being sorry, as neither of us is in the least." I scooted higher in the bed on one elbow and grimaced at the pain. My leg throbbed.

"Need more laudanum?"

"I want to do without it." But I could not.

In the drowsy moments before I slept, I remembered the loss of my fortune—what had Uncle Richard said?

Sometime in the night, I was moved. I knew that I rode in a carriage, I heard Doctor Rillian's voice. I tried to ask a question, but my mouth wouldn't move as I intended.

Joseph's voice rumbled in the distance. "We aren't safe here, Emma. We must go..."

We weren't safe. He would keep me safe.

Hours later, I awoke again, but my eyes refused to stay open. I was being carried. From now on I would go without medicine, come what may.

I slept again for what seemed hours. I am not certain. I woke to sunlight pouring into a rather rustic bedroom of unpainted wooden walls, a quilt of patchwork for a blanket, and a small fire snapping in a nearby grate. An old woman sat in a rocking chair by my side knitting.

"Joseph? Where is Joseph?" How could he have left me?

She offered a smile. "He'll be along soon, I shouldn't wonder."

I tried to raise myself but couldn't. Each limb was a dead weight. My leg throbbed as it had when first wounded. What was happening?

Exhaustion again took hold.

CHAPTER EIGHTEEN

It was days before I even knew where I rested. That afternoon, I waited for Joseph to return and tell me why we'd fled Goodwyn Abbey in the night. The kind older woman ministered to me, a nurse, she'd said. Hired to help while the gentlemen were away. Where had they gone? And why hadn't I been told? I knew the answer, but to be apart from him so soon after we'd been wed hurt to my core.

I sipped more broth and felt as though summer had come upon me with a force. I sweated and tossed and turned, losing my bearings completely. I was sick—in a ship's cabin? Could it be? No. Yet I rocked back and forth, as on the swells of an ocean. When I woke, at least, I thought I was awake, my leg was swollen thick— couldn't move it.

Fevered heat rose, then fell with a chilling sweep of air. Uncle Richard was always forgetting to close the parlor door. A dreadful draft accosted me. Dreadful...

Someone shouted my name. It was all a jumble, I cannot exactly recall, but I did fully awaken after an eternal fever. Joseph and Doctor Rillian sat by my side.

Hands touched my face, gently checked my arms, my legs. "It worked. Her fever is gone."

Joseph peered over me, exhausted and relieved. "Oh Emma. You gave us a fright."

I reached out and he drew me to his chest...

We'd secluded ourselves in a small cottage in Devonshire. Far from Samuel's mad campaign to injure his cousin, my husband, for taking his would-be fortune away from him. Wealth that no longer existed. Did he realize that? He hadn't been caught for his crimes against Zachary, me, and his own father, who had thankfully survived.

Lord Sherborne was doing all in his power to help.

Days passed and I improved, little by little. Joseph read aloud to me some old, familiar tomes. He slept in a cot next to my bed and served me by meeting my every need. I prayed we would have many years of marriage ahead so that I might someday perform the same sacrificial love for him.

One sunny morning, Doctor Rillian urged me to dress and gain some fresh air. The old nurse helped me into a gown. My movements were sluggish, and thankfully, the pain much less.

Joseph helped me walk to the front door of the little cottage. There, before my eyes, was a dream. Was I still sick? Did I remain in a fevered state? Beyond a few hills lay an ocean. Wide, deep, blue. I reached for it as a child might a toy. Was it real or only a mirage?

Joseph carried me in his arms and settled me into a hack chaise. Doctor Rillian placed a picnic basket beside us. "Comfortable?" He wrapped his arm around me as the driver took us to my heart's desire, the place I had always longed to go.

He lifted me out of the chaise and lowered me onto a grassy knoll near the beach and removed my slippers.

"What are you doing?" I had blushed a shade of red without any work of the sun.

"I believe you said that what you wanted most was to feel sand between your toes. Wasn't that your dream?" His brows lifted, offered an intimate smile.

"It is childish."

"It is natural."

"Are you sure?"

"Do you need help with your stockings?"

Yes. That's exactly the help I needed. "I cannot think to expose myself out in the open."

He leaned closer. "We are completely alone."

"Would be a scandal for the heiress to..." No. I was practically a pauper now.

He winked. "What's one more scandal, huh?"

There'd be no arguing with him. I rolled my silks down as modestly as I could.

"I am your husband, Emma." He chuckled. "I am allowed to see your leg. Both of them even."

"I daresay you've already seen it." Ghastly. That wound and the infection...

"You've a beautiful pair." He grinned. "They match perfectly."

I nestled the silks inside my slippers while he took his boots off too. "You aren't the only one with a dream."

He helped me to my feet, wrapping an arm around me, we walked barefooted together to the wet, sandy shore.

The sand...the cool, wet sand. I began to laugh at the foreign sensation. He guided me further to the edge of the water.

"Here, you must get them wet." He pointed at my feet.

The first step, gloriously cool, swished about my toes. Sand filled between them, and slid away with the tide.

Joseph held me close, one arm about my shoulders, his free hand grasping mine. I'd often dreamt of what it must feel like to stand as I did now—only I had no inkling that this one small act could create so much joy in my soul. My new precious link to Joseph snapped the final chain that held me back for so many years. My past no longer suffocated me. Grandfather's over-protective nature could no longer keep me from experiencing goodness. Life. Joseph's grasp on my heart was freeing, hopeful.

I used to think that being happy and fulfilled required entering society to make my debut among the throngs of the wealthy. To dance for the approval of others and bask in the admiration of young gentlemen. Oh no. The good gifts were here, from the hand of God Himself.

His goodness overwhelmed me. I leaned my head against Joseph's chest, listening to the quiet thrum of his heart keeping time with the gentle roar of the ocean.

"Let's take a few more steps," he murmured.

"Will the current carry us away?"

He laughed. "No, love. It won't."

As we went further, water gathered about my ankles. Truly, there was nothing more glorious than this.

"Deeper." His voice rumbled.

The water crept up my calves. Yes, deeper. No more living on the surface waiting for life to happen. No more dreaming and wondering. I would live a true story.

Joseph whispered in my ear. "Perhaps someday I can teach you to swim..."

A new dream took root.

He released me then lifted my chin with his hands. He bent his face to mine and kissed me, then kissed me again. I forgot the sand between my toes, the water about my ankles, and the lapping ocean. Here was fathomless love and I would willingly drown in it.

We stayed at the beach for hours, and true to his word, we weren't bothered by any visitors other than lanky sandpipers.

I would never forget this day, my first taste of sweet freedom. It would be forever emblazoned on my heart as Joseph's laugh mingled with my own. How could it be that the young boy who valiantly saved my life those many years ago would be sealed to my heart forever as my husband?

Had God Himself set the stage in that carriage that we should someday belong to each other? Or was it by circumstances that our lives once again intersected?

For these many years, he had cared about my welfare while I knew nothing of his. Was it by his own valiance—by his dedication to goodness made certain we'd be in each other's paths?

I only knew that whether God used a fated plan or simply allowed the results of our own choices, I was eternally thankful to Him. Maybe one day I would understand how we came to be united as one and how deeply God's goodness reaches. It seemed unsearchable.

Joseph made a fire of driftwood and we nestled beside it, creatures begging for warmth in the waning day.

"You have never been more beautiful than in this moment." A five-o'clock shadow graced his jawline, his gaze smoldered like flames.

"I am a completely soppy sandy mess, my hair has fallen about my shoulders," I flung a wet strand behind my back, "and I might have a sunburn." More likely still flushed from his affections.

"Happy?" He leaned closer.

In truth, I'd never felt wilder or more at ease in my entire life. His lips captured mine again. Perhaps such kisses would one day become commonplace, given we had the rest of our lives to enjoy them. Commonplace perhaps, but I would never grow tired of them, or him. Or his love. Ever...

CHAPTER NINETEEN

I leaned over Joseph's shoulder as he read the missive from Lord Sherborne. His excitement was evident.

"The marriage contract has been found! As well as the signatures in the church register. Everything we need. Praise God."

A wave of relief swept over me. "And Samuel? Have they found him?" I wouldn't rest until the man was behind bars.

Joseph bit his lip. "Still missing. But my uncle is recovering well. That's a bit of good news. Ah, and here is a note from Tessa and Elaina for you." He handed me a folded square.

"For me?" An unexpected pleasure.

"Of course." He winked.

I'd never enjoyed a letter from real friends. But in the haste of my departure and subsequent injury, I was ashamed that this was the first I'd thought of them.

"Is Tessa alright?" She herself might have been in danger. Indeed, Mayfield seemed to overflow with nefarious designs. My heart began to pound. "Please tell me she is safe." Had I not caught a glimpse of her that fateful morning?

Joseph set the letter down and turned to face me. Pulled me onto his lap with his arms wrapped tightly around me. "She is and no danger pursues her."

"You are sure?" Doubt clouded my thoughts.

"Remember, I trained her myself." He kissed my cheek. "I hear she's been quite a help with Cecily in the wake of Zachary's death. Here," he picked up Lord Sherborne's letter, "see for yourself. Tobias has ultimately proven himself worthy. Between Samuel's crime and Zachary's death, he alone stands with honor."

"So Tobias..."

"Is a good egg after all. You might have chosen him."

"Never."

"You're sure?" His brow lifted at the ridiculous question.

Enough silliness. This time, I kissed him in response.

Moments later, he broke away and took my face between his hands. "My dear wife. Sherborne recommends we make our way home."

Home—I had not thought of what home might be. "Wyndhouse?"

"Wyndhouse." He smiled.

Home had always been Chatswick in London. "My uncles. I must write to them."

"Do forgive me, wife, but I wrote to them of our situation but a day after we were married." He quirked a smile. "The London papers are swift to report and I did not want them to needlessly worry."

"That was good of you. Thank you."

I, Lady Emma, was no longer an heiress as there was nothing left to inherit. A fact I had to tell myself again and again. "What will happen to them? What will happen to Chatswick?" Another burning question rose to the surface. "What exactly happened to my fortune?"

"It seems your grandfather wasn't content with his riches. He speculated his fortune in one of Banbury's schemes."

I shook my head. "No. Grandfather would never go near anything with that name."

"There's the rub. He didn't know Banbury was at the top of the scheme or I'm sure you are right. He wouldn't have gone near it."

"But why? His fortune was large enough. More than enough."

"Your uncles say he was only thinking of taking care of you. But his actions backfired."

I let out a puff of air. He wanted more gold—gold that would weigh me down as it had him.

Pieces began to fall into place. "Grandfather must have known." My uncles, too. That day in the breakfast room they read the piece in the newspaper about Banbury. They were planting a story in my mind—and then— "That's why Grandfather had become suddenly urgent to marry me off." It all became clear.

They needed me to marry well before anyone found out about my penniless status. Before the news broke that Lady Bartlett, London's best-kept secret, was nothing to regard after all. Especially when it came to her purse. Poor Mr. Chinworth would have been sorely disappointed to end up with a daughter-in-law such as I, despite his regard for Grandfather. At some level, I had to believe they had my best interests at heart.

Joseph tucked a loose strand of hair back into my chignon. "You are probably right, my sweet wise wife."

Samuel's own devious plotting had been in vain. His life could have been beautiful with a beloved wife and son. But he'd cast it away for the same reason Grandfather sought to keep me safe. Greed for any reason is still greed. A careless waste, a tight-fisted grip. Such vanity.

Despite the greed and plotting around me, here I was: loved and well-wed to Joseph Carter. I could never be sorry for how the Lord had opened – and slammed shut – doors.

He kissed my cheek. "What others intend for evil, God intends for good. You can rest knowing that your grandfather only wanted what was best for you." I gave him a kiss in return.

Days later, a coach waited to take us home. Doctor Rillian had left us the night before to go back to Goodwyn Abbey and back to Matthew Dawes. The generous man wiped a tear when he took his leave. "Mrs. Carter. Do you realize how close you were to losing your leg? I have taken care of many people in my time. Rarely does anyone escape such a serious injury as you have."

"I am grateful to you."

"Me? No, my lady. Every time you look upon your scar, I want you to remember that you have a praying husband. One man's evil designs shall forever signify the miracle God has wrought for you." He winked. "The Good Lord has left you with the full set. He must want you to stand tall—and maybe run now and again. Chase after your future children, mayhap."

Children...

The thought made my heart beat faster.

Joseph handed me into the coach and slid beside me. "Pistols cleaned and ready. But rest assured, we shan't need them."

Strange to travel to the same territory where I'd lived in my infancy. I had so many questions, yet when I thought to ask them, none would tumble from my lips succinctly enough for an answer. I managed merely, "My parents..."

"Yes?" Joseph's eyes softened. He always understood me.

"I..." Truly, I had countless questions but words failed to form.

He took my hand and answered me anyway. "Your mother—she had hair like yours. She was a gentle woman, intelligent. Not given to swooning. She was very kind to me as a boy—always made me feel like I mattered."

I took his memories in like a sponge.

"Your father—you look most like him, my love. He was a good man as far as I knew. He loved your mother—anyone could tell he was smitten with her. He had a reputation for fine horsemanship. And—I recall—he was particularly good to his tenants. Oh, and he was fond of licorice candy. Gave me some each time we met." His smile was wide.

"Mmm." Licorice had always been a favorite of mine.

"You would have loved them." His fingers tightened about mine. "I can take you to visit where you once lived, if you'd like."

"I wondered..."

"Canfell is but three miles from Wyndhouse."

"So close?"

"Indeed. Though the estate was sold not long after the accident, the people living there are congenial. They won't mind letting you see the place."

"That would be lovely."

We traveled onward for a few hours. We both napped. Night had fallen when we arrived, I didn't think my heart could hold more love and hope than it did at that moment. But when Joseph led me to the door of our home, I trembled. My heart burst with gratitude. For here, here was the cottage of my dreams, with windows aglow, curtains fluttering in the breeze. Everything I'd ever wanted – down to the last detail.

Joseph gestured towards a mansion a short distance away. "The original Wyndhouse crumbles, I'm afraid. Dry rot. My father wasn't able to save it, as much as he wanted to. I hope you aren't disappointed?"

"Disappointed?" Tears fell. The cottage was a large one. Not overbearing, it did not boast, yet it stood tall as though it meant to call me closer and then embrace me. I couldn't bear the joy of it. "Even the door is red!" A charming, cheerful color.

"Not what you are accustomed to..."

I clung to him. He quite misunderstood me. "This is the home of my dreams, Joseph. You have no idea how much I've longed for this. Exactly this!"

His eyes captured mine. "You approve?"

"How could I not?"

He bent to lift me as the front door opened and revealed a smiling maid. But the approach of a horse stilled his hands. Gunshots rang through the air.

In a swift movement, Joseph pulled a pistol from its pouch and began to load it. He pushed me to the house. "Get inside—don't come out until I say it's safe."

Another shot fired in the distance.

"Do you think it's Samuel?"

"Could be. Now get inside."

The maid tugged me within.

"To the cellar, Chastity."

"Yes, sir."

She took my hand. "Come, my lady." I could feel her shaking from fear—or did I? She led me down a dimly lit hall—I couldn't wait to explore my new home.

Someone shouted. A man I didn't recognize ran past and through an open door. "Joseph?" Fear clutched my heart.

Another gunshot split the air—another man slipped by, each drawing a rapier.

The maid fell to her knees, terror in her eyes. "What in Heaven's name is going on?"

"Run to the cellar. I'll be right behind you." I couldn't lose Joseph. Not after everything. I needed to see that he was alright...

I pushed through the door and ran after the men. If Samuel was here, exacting revenge, then maybe I might be able to help. How, I didn't know. "Help me, God. Help Joseph." I knew my prayers would be answered.

CHAPTER TWENTY

I followed as best I could—my leg was still weak, but as the good doctor said, I'd need them to run. And I might have to. Sooner than expected. The men disappeared behind Wyndhouse, each circling around the sides. Where was Joseph? Was he alright?

The old structure jutted tall against the dark sky, its stone façade bore a look of having once defended a household and ready to do so again.

A horse stood near the gates, neighing and stamping its hoof, devoid of his master. But I recognized the beast. It *was* Samuel's horse. He'd come to confront us. To kill us. The gunshots announced his arrival.

Surely, he knew by now that I wasn't worth anything to him. Not a single pence. How did he know we'd be here, today of all days? The sky grew darker, the stars, bright when we arrived, dimmed behind clouds.

Men's voices shouted—words indecipherable... Why had Samuel come to this edifice instead of the cottage? Made no sense if he truly wanted to confront Joseph...

A scream rent the air—another shot fired.

"Dear God," I whispered. A sweat broke across my back. "Keep us safe. Protect Joseph."

Footsteps sounded behind me. I turned. A shadowed figure darted to the house but didn't enter.

Heart in my throat, I ran for an old tree stump and sank behind it. Why hadn't I listened to Joseph and stayed in the cellar?

Deep laughter echoed from the mansion. A chop of words followed. "No—don't..." Glass shattered. "Stop!" Another blast of gunfire. Then silence. Deathly silence.

I drew my knees beneath my chin and willed my heart to calm. I needed to think. To reign in my fear. Joseph would be alright. He had to be.

The air stilled— the world held its breath. I rose to my feet. The clouds had revealed the moon that shone directly on Wyndhouse's gaping door. I would go through that entrance—find Joseph. Help him, if need be. I had to know what happened.

It didn't make sense, of course. I didn't have a weapon. But I knew I had to go. Had to find him. If he lay dying, he would know with his final breath that I love him and would gladly die for him, should that help in any way.

Before I could step into the dark house, a pair of arms pulled me away. "Nay, my lady."

I bent and thrust my sharp elbow into his stomach—he released his hold and I plunged to the ground.

"Ooof. Losh, woman. I see Joseph has taught you a thing or two."

Lord Sherborne? "I am so sorry." I trembled at what I'd done. But Joseph would have been proud of my instant reaction.

"Wait here." He stalled me with the flat of his hand. "You must." He handed me a dagger. "Just in case."

I clutched the blade at my side, leaned against the cool stone of the house, and watched him enter.

Joseph's voice rang clear. "Lord Sherborne. Nice of you to drop by." His voice was bright.

"Sorry for the delay, old boy."

My husband yet lived! Thank God.

Joseph spoke again. "You're right on time."

Whispers bounced between the two and in a moment, Joseph was by my side. "Seems I recall directing you to wait in the cellar."

"I thought I could help you."

"Stay here, Emma. And whatever you do, do not come inside. Please." His eyes pleaded. "Isn't safe."

"Is Samuel..."

"Thinks he's hiding, but I know where he is. He won't escape." He looked to the cottage. "If you know what's good for you, you'll return to safety."

"I'll wait." I needed answers. And I didn't want to be far from his side.

More glass crashed. Joseph shook his head. "He thought I still lived here." He pressed a hand to my shoulder. "Stay put, Emma."

The moment Joseph stepped back inside, Samuel shouted. "Don't move. Stay where you are, cousin. My pistol is cocked, ready to fire if you move one iota."

I heard the crunch of glass beneath Joseph's boots. "Samuel. How nice of you to pay us a visit."

"I see Wyndhouse is in pristine condition. Too bad your mock heiress can't restore your fortunes. Poor cousin." He snorted. "You always were the poor, poor cousin."

"There are other riches than gold, Samuel."

"You sound like the vicar."

"Didn't know you ever listened to the sermons. Should have paid more attention."

"Little good they did me."

"Why are you here? Emma is no longer your concern."

"You ruined me. *She* ruined me. Posing as an heiress to tempt me. Spend *my* fortune to entice her. They are all like that, cousin. They tempt you, steal from you. All a pretense to get what they want."

Joseph remained patient. "What do you suppose they want?"

"What you have. Your money. Not you, no. Never *you*. Never true love, though I hoped for it. Once."

"But there is true love, Samuel." Joseph remained bold in his words.

"You just wait and see. Actually. Maybe you won't wait and see before the night is over. I intend on sparing you the misery of being used."

"Used? Are you speaking of your first wife?"

"So you know about her." He took a breath. "She got what she deserved."

"Whatever did she do to you?"

"What does every woman on this stinking planet do? Betrayed me! Cheated on me! I loved her and she *trampled my soul into the filth.*"

"And the child?"

"The boy." Bitterness laced his words. "I don't even know if the child is mine. But he has died, hasn't he? Good riddance to the wicked pair."

"He isn't dead."

"What do you mean?"

"He's been hidden for safe-keeping. From you."

"You think I would kill the brat?" He scoffed.

"I overheard as such. Your brother—"

"My brother is dead because of you! And for that, I will end your life and hers. Zachary wasn't supposed to die."

"Neither am I, Samuel. Neither of us are supposed to die today. God put us on this earth to live and know His love for us."

"Love—" He spat. "You can go straight to that God of love and"—a loud crack sounded—like several twigs snapping at once, grinding, scraping, crashing in a great shift of woodwork, glass, and stone. The house was crumbling with shattering force.

The stone vibrated and I screamed though could not be heard above the sounds of destruction. Dust blew from the door and smashed windows. My vision blurred, I coughed, choking.

"Joseph! Lord Sherborne!" I tried to shout but my voice crackled, too quiet to be heard. The wait was brief. The pair stumbled through the door, dusty, but unscathed. 'Twas over in a moment.

"What happened?" I did my best to wipe the dust away from Joseph's shining eyes.

"The marble stairway was too heavy for the rotted support beam. Finally gave way." He brushed debris from his hair.

Lord Sherborne tossed his cravat to the ground along with his outer jacket.

"We need to dig him out of the rubble." Joseph was determined.

"I'll be shocked if he survived." Lord Sherborne pulled his vest off next.

Joseph followed suit. "Your arrival was timely."

"The reprobate's been hiding out in my garden maze. Callum chased him out, but not after he overheard me talking to Elaina. That's how he knew you'd returned. My apologies, Carter."

"Never mind that."

One of the men I'd seen running from the cottage rounded the mansion. "He's the only one here, Carter." He uncocked his pistol. "That was quite a smash-up. Glad we didn't go inside."

"Indeed." Joseph nodded. "Thank you for your assistance."

"We knew you weren't training anyone at present. Seemed suspicious."

"Stay for another few minutes, will you? Help me dig my cousin from the rubble." Joseph turned to me. "Go back to the cottage, love. Have Chasity start tea. We'll be there shortly."

He stopped and turned back around. "Oh, and do have a pallet made for Samuel. Just in case." He turned to his friend. "Run for the doctor—good lad."

I stumbled to the cottage and back through the cheerful red door. It wasn't until I'd reached the kitchen that I realized that I still clutched the dagger. The worst might nearly have happened. Might have...but did not.

The maid called Chasity peered from behind the cellar door. "Free to come out, then, my lady?" Her eyes widened as she spied the dagger. "Good gracious, what have you been up to?" She stepped back as I tossed the dagger to the butcher block, glad to be rid of it.

Not a half hour later, Joseph, Lord Sherborne, and the few young men who had come to help carried Samuel's still form on a stretcher into the house. Covered in white dust and dark smudges, his body was broken. Crushed. His limbs were mangled. Blood oozed from a head wound. They settled him onto the pallet we'd made before the low kitchen fire.

"He lives, but barely." Joseph's mouth drew a grim line.

Lord Sherborne wiped grime from his hands with a towel. "Your uncle is hours from arriving. When he heard that Samuel had been found, nothing would stop him."

Throughout the long night, we watched our assailant dying before our eyes in the care of those who might have loved him if he'd allowed it—ah. Such waste. What a loss. The good life he might have lived...

Mr. Chinworth arrived with torrential rains. When the door opened, it looked as though he'd wept with the skies. Only at that moment did he discover that his son wasn't long for this earth.

I couldn't help but wonder that he should bother to see – to touch –the son who nearly murdered him. All because of his wicked desire for an early inheritance.

Grave and thin from the overdose, Mr. Chinworth knelt by Samuel's side, chin quivering. He placed light hands over his son's form. "Samuel...Samuel..." Tears continued falling.

Samuel opened his eyes for the first time since the house collapsed upon him. His lips moved, but no words formed.

Mr. Chinworth leaned closer. "I'm here, son."

But why would he want to be? Why wasn't he angry? Or ready to finish him off? A surge of fury boiled deep within me. Samuel's evil had caused great difficulty and grief. I wavered between being sorry for the brute's pain and the idea that he deserved what he was getting.

Samuel's lips moved again. "Dying..."

Again, Mr. Chinworth hovered over his son's face. "I'm here. I love you."

How could he love him? How?

"Don't...don't love me..." His eyes misted.

"I should have been a better father."

Samuel's lips moved again, "I—sorry. Sorry. Tell—sorry." Tears left smudged trails down his filthy skin. "God—God—"

"Go to God, son. He will love you best."

Blood trickled from his lips and he shuddered, then stilled.

I'd never before seen a grown man weep. Mr. Chinworth, in spite of Samuel's sins, wept over his broken form as though he'd lost someone good and deeply beloved. Indeed, I felt unworthy to stand and watch. A broken son being ushered into the arms of another broken Son.

Was this the love of God? That He would go through any lengths to reveal the bold truth of His love—even to the point of pulling a house down upon him? Is that why I endured a life without parents, so that I might reach for God as my Father? That at every turn, from the glory of a sandy beach to the sudden lurch of a crashing carriage—we are tossed into an opportunity to know this Truth above all?

My knees weakened. Our lives would be prodded by Him until we recognized the meaning of a Father's love.

I swallowed, shamed at my willingness to deprive Samuel of what he needed most.

Joseph took my hand and led me upstairs. He poured a cup of tea. "Rest, my love."

I leaned into his chest and wept as Mr. Chinworth's great sobs filled the halls.

CHAPTER TWENTY-ONE

I found that I had indeed slept. When I woke, I was still fully clothed atop my bed. Joseph burrowed beside me, his arm draped around my waist. I'd curved into his warmth. Yawning, I turned to face him and he blinked awake.

He stroked my cheek. "I wanted your homecoming to be...romantic...carry you over the threshold." He shrugged.

"You can do the honors every day hereafter."

"I'll take you up on that. Rest assured."

"How is your uncle?" So many tragedies.

"Grieving. Two sons gone, in such a short time."

"Such a waste. If only I had stayed in London as you begged me to do—" His finger pressed against my lips, silencing my next words.

"Their choices aren't your fault." He sat up and eased off the bed. "Uncle wants to talk to us before he leaves. Plans to take Samuel's body back for burial. He needs to depart soon if he is to make Butterton by nightfall." He sighed. "I'll ring for tea."

We made our way to a small library. Despite last night's pain, a little swell of joy rose within me. My new abode felt more like a home than anything I'd ever known.

Mr. Chinworth paced before the fireplace, eyes red, a knotted handkerchief dangling from one hand. "I don't know how to tell you…" He took a breath and sat. "I knew your Grandfather had lost his fortune before you came to us, Emmaline."

My lips parted—he knew? And he waited until now to tell me. Why?

"I regret that I misled my sons into thinking you an heiress—as indeed, you believed you were." He rubbed his hands together. "Your grandfather and I had hoped that you'd make a swift match and avoid any uncomfortable change of circumstances."

"So I've gathered." Perhaps they did have my best interests at heart.

"I wanted at least one of my boys to be settled—and—" his face flushed. "I—" sweat dripped from his brow.

Still, the admission confused. I had to ask. "It is unusual to be such good friends as to take on a penniless gentlewoman." Especially within society. I bit my lip. "It was strange to hear your name for the first time a few months ago. If you were so close to my grandfather, why hadn't I heard of you before? Why have you not come to visit?"

Mr. Chinworth shrugged. "I owed him. Everything."

Joseph stepped closer. "Define everything."

He took a ragged breath and looked me square in the eye. "Because your parents' deaths were my fault."

The air left the room. His admission hung thick, I couldn't breathe.

"Explain." Joseph's voice had grown cold. Ominous.

"I realized it wasn't fair that you'd lost so much already." He pressed a fist to his middle. "It's been eating at me these twenty years. Twenty years!" His voice boomed. "I had to do something! When I got wind that your grandfather had been deceived by Banbury, I knew I had a chance to redeem myself." He laughed at the irony. "Only I've found that people can't redeem themselves. Only God can bring about such changes."

Joseph flicked his head and gritted his teeth. "You still haven't explained, Uncle." His ire grew.

"Alright! I will unburden." He shouted. "It was Banbury. It was always Banbury. Only I didn't know he was using a pseudonym."

I licked my lips. "What does Banbury—or you—have to do with the carriage accident that killed my parents?"

"Bets were laid." He mumbled.

Bets?

"Speak up, Uncle."

"Bets were laid on one more race. The first carriage to pass through the village of Banbury's choice would be chased down. The drivers were complicit. Upstanding gentlemen posed as highwaymen and would halt the carriage after a good run, then strip the interior of its valuables. The kitty would then be divided amongst us." He swallowed and whispered, "No one was supposed to die. Was all fun and games, you see. Fun and games. Nothing more." His eyes looked blank.

Joseph folded his arms. "Lady Bartlett's diamonds were still in the carriage when the magistrate returned to the scene. But Emma's never seen them. I wonder why that is."

"No one was supposed to die. That wasn't part of the bargain." He avoided Joseph's question.

"Why would you play such a wicked game?"

I wondered at Joseph's cool tone, knowing the years he'd spent trying to unravel the event—trying to make sense of what he'd seen, and the grief of watching my parents die – for nothing – it now appeared. He'd endured threat after threat, been beaten for trying. Since the start, the answer had always been closer to home. Much too close to home.

"Grandfather told me that you saved him from drowning in the Thames. That Banbury had pushed him in—and—."

"The man tricked me. I didn't know it was him. I would never have dealt with such a man."

Joseph gestured with one hand. "I ask again, why would you join such a wicked game?"

Mr. Chinworth wiped more sweat from his forehead. "It's true. I lay the highest bet that day. I didn't know Lord and Lady Bartlett were within. Or you, nephew."

Joseph continued his questioning. "And you—were you one of the highwaymen chasing us?"

He paled. Ah...the answer at last.

"The same man who abandoned an innocent family when the carriage careened from the ledge?"

Inconceivable. Was it true?

"Yes. I am guilty of murder." His words were the final coffin nails.

"My grandfather—and uncles. They didn't know?" My voice sounded small. "Never knew?" I feared the answer.

He shook his head.

"If they had..."

Joseph wasn't finished. "You paid off the magistrate, didn't you? You knew I sought answers. Truth."

Mr. Chinworth pointed a finger at Joseph. "I never told them to beat you up."

"How did you know I was beaten?"

"Your father must have told me."

"We told no one."

Mr. Chinworth, the tall, once handsome man, sank to his knees and reached a hand into his coat.

Joseph sprung to action and wrested both arms around his back. I wished for a rope to tie up the villain.

"I have no weapon, I promise you." Mr. Chinworth wept openly. "I only mean to see my confession through."

Joseph released his hold and searched Mr. Chinworth's coat. "You may continue."

He handed me an inlaid wooden box. "Your mother's diamonds. I wasn't about to let Banbury get his paws on them. And I didn't dare return them to your grandfather or he might have suspected my involvement."

But that didn't explain why he took them in the first place. I stared at the man.

"I repent of what I've done, Emmaline Carter. I don't expect you to forgive me. Either of you. But I couldn't go on—" He broke again. "I couldn't go on. I had a wife and sons that needed me..."

The scene from last night replayed in my mind. A father sending his broken son to the only One who might heal him, body and soul. I had to do the same. I had to leave this man to God.

Lord Sherborne came from behind a bookshelf. He'd heard everything. "Chinworth. You do understand that I will need to turn you over to the magistrate? However, I will allow Samuel's body to be delivered to Mayfield first."

He nodded. "I want to pay for what I've done." He rose to his feet. "I despise the whole of it. Tobias can see to compensation. I...and the child. What of my grandchild? He is missing and has not been found."

Joseph startled. "He was hidden for safekeeping—was he not?"

Lord Sherborne folded his arms, his face grim. "I'm afraid he has been kidnapped. We haven't been able to ascertain his whereabouts for a few weeks."

"Who would do such a thing?" My question hung in the air.

Chinworth's eyes watered, his chin trembled. "I was a fool in my youth. A fool. Gained the world only to lose my soul."

Lord Sherborne led him from the room and oversaw the departure. Joseph pulled me beside him on the settee, his arm about me. We sat in silence for quite some time, my mother's diamonds between us.

I picked up the box and unlatched the closure. Diamonds did indeed rest within. Two necklaces, a bracelet, a ring. Sparkling. Brilliant. And more. A tiny bunch of baby's hair, tied with a silk ribbon, sewn onto parchment. In faded ink, I read, *"My darling's feather-soft baby hair, 1789. How she grows, how I love her..."*

Joseph's voice wavered with emotion as he held me tighter. "True wealth..." The diamonds fell to the side as we embraced.

We had found our treasure.

Epilogue

The gloom of that day lifted with the sunrise. For all the sorrow we'd witnessed, the new joys facing us were incomparable. The cottage was truly the home of my heart's dreams. Along with the cozy abode, it came ready-made with a small crew of caring servants.

The grounds boasted a training gym, built from a repurposed barn adjacent to the garden. A few young men lived in a smaller cottage, also worked there in exchange for the training Joseph offered them for six months out of the year. And when they left, a new group of young men would take their place.

Another blessing, the vast grounds of Wyndam's estate were more beautiful even than that of Mayfield. Joseph had plans—big plans—to see the farmland successful, apart from his self-reliance instruction for eager young men.

After a few weeks, we made our way to London to visit the solicitor. I signed papers and cut my losses. Said my warm goodbyes to Chatswick, and my Uncle Richard.

The man couldn't fathom economizing – or caring for himself – and promptly made a marriage proposal to Mrs. Norris, of all people! They married within a fortnight, leaving Uncle Gerald very unaccustomed to living by himself.

Uncle Gerald smirked. "Your Uncle Richard is more the romantic than I gave him credit for. Indeed. Left me quite alone."

"Come live with us." I offered.

Joseph nodded approval.

Uncle Gerald sniffed, having left his egg grow cold and his tea colder. "Might I help teach the boys?" He looked hopeful.

Joseph's brows rose, amused. "I'm sure there will be something you can do. I'm certain of it."

"Indeed. I feel as giddy as a schoolboy. Haven't been out and about enough, you know? One gets cabin fever. I do believe the countryside will suit me. Yes, indeed." He swallowed some tea and ate his eggs.

Uncle Gerald and I linked arms and toured Chatswick one last time, room by room, memory by memory. We finally came to Grandfather's. Had he been unwittingly poisoned by the dangerous elixir? We would never know. Like much of my past, I had to put those questions to rest. He was in God's hands now.

Uncle Gerald motioned to a closet. "Oh, I almost forgot. The renters will not want these, but perhaps you do?" He opened the doors. Hanging within were portraits. Large and beautifully framed.

"Who?" But I already knew. God's ways were truly mysterious.

"Why, your parents." He smiled. "They loved you dearly."

Joseph's hand slipped around mine, squeezed tight.

"This I know."

About the Author

Ann Elizabeth Fryer loves nothing more than using story and romance to relay the depths and graciousness of a Father who holds us securely in the palms of His hands. Ann, her husband, and three children make their home in small-town Illinois where they can hear church bells keep time and tradition.

Visit her website at annelizabethfryer.com

The Hearts Unlocked Collection:

Of Needles and Haystacks

Of Horse and Rider

Of Hearts and Home

Of Time and Circumstance

Of Pens and Ploughshares

Butterton Brides Series:

A Convenient Sacrifice

A Favorable Match

An Opportune Proposal, coming January 2024

Printed in Dunstable, United Kingdom